To Tyrone.

& George

With Love

From

Peter Congdon

SUFFER THE LITTLE CHILDREN

Peter Congdon

MINERVA PRESS
ATLANTA LONDON SYDNEY

SUFFER THE LITTLE CHILDREN
Copyright © Peter Congdon 1999

All Rights Reserved

No part of this book may be reproduced in any form
by photocopying or by any electronic or mechanical means,
including information storage or retrieval systems,
without permission in writing from both the copyright owner
and the publisher of this book.

ISBN 0 75410 811 2

First Published 1999 by
MINERVA PRESS
315–317 Regent Street
London W1R 7YB

Printed in Great Britain for Minerva Press

've # SUFFER THE LITTLE CHILDREN

*This book is dedicated to my wife, Mary
and my four children,
Joseph, Rachel, Edward and Andrea.*

About the Author

Dr Peter Congdon is a consultant educational psychologist. He has many years of experience both as a qualified teacher and as an educational psychologist working for local authorities. Dr Congdon has addressed many national and international conferences on the subjects of gifted, dyslexic and left-handed children. He is the founder and director of the Gifted Children's Information Centre in Solihull and has spent many years studying the development of literacy skills in young children. Dr Congdon was awarded his doctorate by London University as a result of research in this area. He has written numerous articles on gifted, dyslexic and left-handed children as well as those who suffer from Attention Deficit/Hyperactivity disorder. Dr Congdon is the author of *Phonic Skills and Their Measurement* (Pub. Basil Blackwell) and the new *Ant to Zip* series which is a structured phonic programme for teaching reading, spelling and handwriting to all children and especially to those with specific learning difficulty/dyslexia.

Acknowledgements

The inspiration behind this book is based on the lives of many former professional colleagues, friends and associates in the North Warwickshire area. I acknowledge them all but in particular pay tribute to Sheila Denney and Philippa Dicker.

In proof-reading and in preparing the manuscript for the publisher I am indebted to the painstaking and meticulous work of my friend, George Tregaskis.

Foreword

Suffer the Little Children is based on the work and experiences of the author who, as an educational psychologist, was employed in the Nuneaton area of North Warwickshire for a period of eighteen years. The name Nuneaton arose from the town's original foundation which was believed to be that of a nunnery. Likewise in the story the name of the fictional borough of Monaston is said to have evolved from its association with a monastic foundation. Names of districts and villages in and around Nuneaton find their parallels in the story. Hartshill becomes Goose Common, Milby becomes Hatley and the neighbouring towns of Bedworth and Atherstone become Duckingford and Baverstone respectively. It is to be stressed that characters, incidents and episodes in the story are largely composite in nature. Whilst they are based on real events and personalities and in some cases names may be similar to those of actual colleagues or acquaintances in the author's experience, changes have been made in order to retain the essential fictional quality of the work.

Apart from entertainment value, a central purpose of the story is to make a contribution towards popularising an understanding of child psychology through the medium of fiction or drama. Inevitably some technical terms or psychological jargon infiltrate the work and in order to help the reader in this respect a glossary has been included.

Peter Congdon

Contents

Song		11
One	Monaston: A Religious Foundation	13
Two	It's a Picasso!	24
Three	Riddler on the Roof	53
Four	The Kiss of Life	88
Five	A Case of Asperger's Syndrome	114
Six	A Boxing Tournament	143
Seven	Lunch at Harry's	173
Eight	The Baverstone Ball Game	205
Glossary		236

Song

Suffer the little children
And let them come to thee
For we were little children
Upon our mother's knee
But many of those children
They suffer agony
So suffer the little children
And let them come to thee.
Suffer the little children
And guide them through their life
They understand so little
Of evil, sin and strife
But as they grow much older
Help them that we must
Or those same little children
Will never in us trust.
Suffer the little children
Part of God's family
Our future is our children
To keep us safe and free
But many of those children
Need love and sympathy
So suffer the little children
And let them come to thee.

Peter Congdon

Chapter One
Monaston: A Religious Foundation

Monaston is a place which exists basically for the residents. It has few attractions for tourists or visitors. Within its boundaries was once an ancient monastery, the town's name and origin. Today no one is sure exactly where the monastery was located. It remains a matter of speculation, although the local curator of the borough's museum has clear ideas on the subject.

During the industrial revolution Monaston grew in importance and size as rich coal seams were discovered in the area. Mines were named after the districts in which they were located. Within the town itself but situated near its periphery are three main mines. These are Sockton, Dampstone and Goose Common.

In the 1960s Monaston had a population of about forty thousand souls. This gradually grew in the following decade as the town became a dormitory for larger urbanisations within the region. Like many industrial towns, Monaston had, and still has, its share of poverty.

During the early 1970s the town was designated a priority area by the Labour Government of the day. At that time some examples of its poverty could fairly be described as bordering on the abject. Individuals who appeared reasonably clothed and fed and who were unremarkable on the street might nevertheless spend their domestic lives in stone hovels which lacked, in some cases, both sanitation and furniture, and where they had nothing to sleep on but a pile of rags. Such were the condemned dwellings of districts which had not yet arrived in the twentieth century. Surprisingly enough, a number of examples of such dwellings were located in a district which rejoiced in the exotic name of Paradise Village.

Apart from a famous Victorian authoress, Monaston boasted no outstanding names in its history. It did, however, lay claim to certain well-known families who appeared unique to the town and who had lived there for many generations. The reputation of such families, whilst often newsworthy, was not always of the virtuous kind.

On its periphery at a place known as Ruff Hollow, Monaston had a large gypsy encampment. Like many such places, its very existence was a bone of contention with local residents. The number of children in the encampment was such that the local authority had created a special unit in one of its schools in order to meet the educational needs of the travellers' offspring.

Although from a local government standpoint Monaston was part of a greater county area and a number of its officers were county appointments, it was nevertheless a borough in its own right and, as such, enjoyed some autonomy. It had its own mayor and its own council, and many important decisions concerning the welfare of the town were made in the imposing Victorian Town Hall, a monument to civic pride suitably located in the town centre.

Like many small county towns, Monaston had its weekly market, which in this case had an ancient history. Some of the elders of the borough could recall children playing barefoot in the market place and women fighting over goods, stripped to the waist, in the early part of the century.

Monaston had its annual carnival, its local newspaper and its own football team, appropriately nicknamed the Monks. Although the latter never aspired to any of the major leagues, it nevertheless drew respect within the region and had, over the years, consistently acted as a useful nursery club for a number of players who later made their debut with more well-known professional clubs.

Our story begins in the Town Hall itself. Located in the town centre, the Town Hall was, and still is, an imposing Victorian building, possibly a little large and over-extravagant when one considers the size of Monaston. The Town Hall is the setting of our drama, and its principal protagonists are the professional, secretarial and maintenance staff of one department of the institution, namely the Schools Psychological Service.

At the head of the department were two area educational psychologists. Technically both were county appointments and were on an equal footing, although one was considerably senior in age and had worked in the Monaston area for many years alone before being joined by a colleague as the service developed. Owing to his seniority, it was not surprising that Dr Wilcox, who had become something of an institution in Monaston, was sometimes regarded as the head of the department by local head teachers as well as by secretarial and other administrative staff.

Dr Wilcox, or Harry, as he was affectionately called by many, was an unusual and, to some extent, unknown quantity. A non-medical doctor of philosophy, rumour had it that he had begun his working life in business but, not over-ingratiated with finance and materialism, he had gravitated to teaching and later, with the acquisition of various degrees and diplomas, had become a fully qualified educational psychologist. Harry was one of those rare specimens who could be funny, intelligent and popular at the same time. He was essentially a free spirit and, unlike many educational psychologists, his attitudes towards certain subjects were little influenced by the attitudes of his employees. From time to time, Harry would appear in immaculate dress in which everything matched, down to the triangle of his handkerchief peeping above his pocket. On such occasions, the buzz would go round the office that Flash Harry was around.

When Harry spoke, he did so with authority and sometimes had people sitting on the edge of their seats. His sense of humour included the double entendre and his remarks were sometimes punctuated with glittering phrases. He was capable of making grave, statesmanlike utterances on comparatively insignificant subjects. He was also well aware of the gravitational pull of good stories and he had plenty of these up his sleeve. Harry referred to them as sociological anecdotes rather than stories.

Harry Wilcox was a single man and probably always had been so. He was in his late forties. Although little was known of his background, he was strongly believed to have an interesting pedigree. Harry appeared to have two distinct lives. There was his professional employment as an educational psychologist and there was his personal and private life. His address was a cottage in the grounds of Hackford Hall, the residence of the Earl of Beersford and his family. Harry, who sometimes referred to the earl as 'Old Beerie', did not appear to be an ordinary resident on the estate. In the first place, he was a doyen, or important person, in the local hunt. He was in fact a joint master. Although Harry was largely reticent about the exact details of his background, it would appear that he had had a public school education; his accent and extrovert, self-confident air sometimes held testimony to the fact. He also, on occasion, but not apparently deliberately so, dropped names of important gentry with whom he seemed to rub shoulders.

Harry was a connoisseur of art, although he openly admitted that he couldn't draw a teapot himself. His taste was catholic but he had a particular love of the Victorian masters. Hanging on the wall in his office was a framed print of Diego Velázquez's *Las Meniñas* (The Ladies in Waiting), a painting regarded by many as the greatest in the world. Harry seldom lost the opportunity to draw the attention of any new visitor to his office to the copy of the masterpiece and explain to them why the picture was held in such high esteem. 'The work gives you the extraordinary sense of being somewhere else,' he would say. 'In fact you feel that you are actually in the artist's studio.' Harry had many virtues but he also had one shortcoming which the secretarial staff found aggravating. Despite his relatively high salary, he was seldom punctual in paying his dues. When asked for his weekly contribution to the tea money, he would frequently complain that he was 'suffering from a deficiency of pecuniary assets in the form of small change'.

Harry's colleague, who formed the other half of the educational psychological team, was Bruce Whitford. Bruce was originally from the south-west of England and retained a strong Devonian accent. He had only recently been appointed to the newly-created post in Monaston, and hitherto had worked in the London area. Like Harry, he was a committed professional. Bruce was in his early thirties and was married to Marie, a former state-registered nurse. They had three small children and were in the process of transferring home from the suburbs of London to the Midlands. Both Bruce and his wife were looking forward to the move since they felt that, with a growing family, they would now be able to afford a larger house, since property in the Midlands was cheaper than in the south-east of England and Bruce's recent promotion to a senior post meant a higher income.

Like many psychologists, Bruce enjoyed specialising in certain areas. The subject of his Master's degree had been the development of phonic skills in young children and, in conjunction with this, he had put together a literacy programme for teaching dyslexic children. The programme was entitled 'Ant to Zip' and it involved a carefully structured step-by-step approach to teaching the skills of reading, writing and spelling simultaneously so that one would reinforce the other. Bruce felt that his landing of the new senior post in Monaston was largely, if not exclusively, due to the fact that he had impressed his interviewers with his knowledge of dyslexia, a common disability of people who have special difficulty with reading and spelling. Eventually Bruce hoped to pursue his researches into the area in order to obtain a doctorate.

A very important third arm of the School's Psychological Service, and sometimes regarded as Harry Wilcox's sidekick, was Delia Berry, a qualified psychiatric social worker. Hers was an unusual appointment as she was the only one of her kind appointed directly by the education department. During the early 1970s the vast majority of social workers were employed by, and came under, the auspices of the newly-created Department for Social Services. However, Delia preserved a much valued independence from that. She undoubtedly enjoyed certain advantages in having administrative superiors who themselves lacked a social work background.

Delia was married to Canon Berry, a Church of England clergyman who held a post of dual responsibility. He was the parish priest in the local village where the Berrys lived and he also held the important post of administrator for all the Church of England schools in the region. Such a post gave him a key position on the County Education Committee and thereby contact with many important local government officials, a situation which Delia was ready to exploit from time to time. The Berrys appeared to be happily married although career-wise they went their separate ways. Both were so busy that, as Delia once put it, the only time they met was in bed. They had four children, three of whom were grown up and the youngest, a boy, was coming towards the end of his secondary school education.

Although based in the Monaston area and using rooms in various offices, Delia's remit was countywide. She was known for the way she raced around the countryside from one destination to another at cartoon-like speeds. From time to time Delia was capable of making a remark or taking an action which would incur the wrath of certain individuals or even whole departments, to the extent that formal complaints would be made or communication would break down for a period. This normally happened with other professionals but seldom with clients. Such a state of affairs, however, was never permanent since Delia would normally bide her time and then restore relationships by means of an unexpected phone call or visit in which she would adopt an air as if nothing untoward had ever happened.

If there was one thing which Delia had plenty of, it was energy. Whenever there was something unpleasant to carry out, the team invariably turned to her. She was a busybody in every sense of the word. Her work was her life and yet somehow she had managed to raise a family of four children without her career seeming to be affected. Much of Delia's work, such as visiting families, was carried out during the evenings when fathers would normally be at home. Consequently her reports during case conferences always held great interest since she was often privy to background information which was not normally available to other professionals. With such knowledge Delia could sometimes throw a whole new light on a situation, and she never lost an opportunity of so doing.

Apart from the two psychologists and their psychiatric social worker, Delia Berry, a number of other professionals were familiar visitors to the department. These included members of the Education Welfare Service who were the successors of the former School Board officers whose duty it was to ensure that all children of statutory age attended school. Although their main task was still to ensure school attendance, the new breed of education welfare officer, or EWO as they were often referred to, was more akin to the job of a social worker. Monaston had a strong team of EWOs and the area, unlike many underprivileged districts, had developed one of the most successful school attendance records in the country. Some argued that the success was partly due to the nature of the area which lacked the presence of a truant's paradise such as the gravitational pull of the tubes in London or the dockland in Liverpool.

The SPS (as the Schools Psychological Service tended to be called) had the services of three hard-working secretaries. Their office or typing pool was quite spacious, and was normally a hub of activity. It was often used as a meeting place or rendezvous where professionals chatted or discussed matters which they shared and which were not demanding of too much confidentiality. They frequently did this while sipping coffee.

Irene Cathcart was the senior secretary. Tall, sedate and never without her spectacles, she appeared to have her fingers in a multitude of pies simultaneously. Quiet, precise but definite in speech, Irene was the soul of tact. In periods of crisis she could preserve a calm dignity when all about her were losing theirs. She was in her mid-forties and had never married. Instead she appeared to be wedded to her work and in particular to seeing that all Dr Wilcox's administrative and secretarial needs were met punctually and efficiently. Irene lived with and cared for an elderly father who suffered from Parkinson's disease. It was believed that her domestic problems were quite onerous, although she seldom complained of them. Many offices

Their office or typing pool was normally a hub of activity.

have a central figure who, whilst it is not immediately obvious, seems to act as an anchor or steadying influence. This was Irene Cathcart's role in the SPS.

In contrast to Irene, the other two secretaries, Tina Duplock and Donna Bence, were both lively, chatty and in their twenties. Donna, the younger and more verbose of the two, was a great reader of the tabloids and followed most of the soaps on television. She was something of a motor-mouth and was sometimes referred to as 'the News of the World' or more cruelly on one occasion by a senior member of staff as 'Rent-a-Gob'. Her current boyfriend worked in a local bakery. Donna was a recent appointment, having just completed a secretarial course at the local technical college. Industrious in her way and full of enthusiasm, her typing often exposed spelling mistakes, and Harry Wilcox had wondered whether she, in fact, had a degree of dyslexia, although no one had had the courage as yet to suggest it to her. Donna was also left-handed and, when taking notes, habitually hooked her hand around the top of the writing paper as is the wont of many sinistrals or left-handers.

Tina, who was some three years older than Donna, was somewhat less garrulous and certainly more discreet. She was a good listener and when she expressed surprise she did so with an O-shaped mouth reminiscent of Edvard Munch's painting, *The Scream*. Tina had once been engaged to a member of the local fire brigade and to celebrate the occasion, members of the department had clubbed together and bought her a not inexpensive engagement present. However, the relationship was subsequently broken off and the subject was no longer mentioned, at least in the office. Like Donna, Tina was a product of a local secondary school and had achieved her secretarial qualification at the Monaston Technical College. She was always neatly dressed but sometimes in the winter wore high leather boots which seemed to force her into the gait of a newborn giraffe.

Finally there was Arthur Brown, a popular, corpulent and jovial character in his early forties who, strictly speaking, did not work in the SPS department as such but who provided a useful link between the Educational Administration staff and the SPS. Arthur had sundry responsibilities, including schools' furniture, caretakers, provision of special equipment for handicapped children and checking out letters from teachers who were absent on account of obscure illnesses. Arthur was often seen in the corridors of the Town Hall in his shirt sleeves and capacious trousers, sporting a colourful tie as he carried important documents from one room to another. Many offices have an Arthur, someone who is full of practical jokes, who may be seen whispering to secretaries or waylaying a colleague with the latest funny story. Arthur Brown had wide sporting interests. He still played table tennis and never missed the football pools or taking his occasional holiday to coincide with Cheltenham Races. At Christmas it was Arthur who arranged the office party and any other jocular activities which accompanied it.

Chapter Two
It's a Picasso!

Bruce Whitford had only been in Monaston once before and that was on the occasion of his interview for the newly-created post of a second area educational psychologist. Until then Harry Wilcox had covered the whole area himself. Bruce had arrived by train for his interview and left less than three hours later, having had little opportunity to see even the centre of the borough. Today, however, was different. It was a sunny Sunday afternoon in early September in the year 1971. Bruce was travelling by car and heading for a small hotel in the middle of Monaston, where he had arranged to live for a short time as a preliminary to finding a new home for his family. As the car sped through the suburbs, Bruce felt a sense of peace – the existence of an easier way of life, less pressure. Little did he know, however, that in those houses which he was passing life could be as vibrant and pulsating as any in the large metropolis.

Bruce entered the town from the south-east side where the trunk road soon merged into ribbon development and suburbia. The houses, many of them detached, with spacious gardens in front, pleased him. He imagined the possibility of one day being able to purchase such a property, although he did realise that the scenario was a little unrealistic in the near future. The district on this peaceful Sunday afternoon also gave Bruce something of a false impression of what life was really like in Monaston. The relatively small Butterworth and Mutley residential area was hardly representative of the mining town itself, which in the early Seventies still had its fair share of poverty and deprivation.

Bruce soon found the hotel where he was to spend his first night. It was small, cosy and had a friendly atmosphere. That evening he dined at the hotel, went for a brief walk around the town centre, rang his family to assure them that all was well and retired early.

Bruce arrived at the Town Hall about 9 a.m. the next day. He was greeted by two uniformed men at the main entrance. They were council employees who took it in turn to chauffeur the mayor of Monaston and other dignitaries to their various civic duties and, when not doing this, they could be found in the office near the entrance of the Town Hall where they served other functions, which included showing visitors where the various departments were located. Bruce vaguely recollected the location of the education department from the time of his interview. However, today it was confirmed for him by one of the uniformed gentlemen.

For such a small borough, the Town Hall was quite awe-inspiring. Victorian in origin, it had three storeys and four entrances. Access to the main entrance was up a series of steps. Through the main entrance one came to the reception and information desk, to the left of which was a grand staircase leading to the first floor where the council chamber and mayor's parlour and other grandiose rooms were located. The Education department, along with the Health department and Rates office, was located on the ground floor. Bruce had a distinct feeling of importance as he walked down one of the corridors of this imposing building with its typically Victorian decor and many portraits of famous local personalities. It contrasted sharply with the terrapin structure attached to a local primary school where he had been based in his last post.

The door was open to the secretary's office of the Schools Psychological Service. Bruce was expected and Irene Cathcart, the senior member of the typing pool, welcomed him.

'Dr Wilcox is in his room,' she exclaimed, pointing to one of the doors leading off the main office. 'Do go through.'

Bruce knocked and simultaneously opened the door.

'Welcome Bruce,' said Harry Wilcox, rising from his chair in front of a desk, the top of which was effectively hidden by numerous documents and was well known for being in a state of terminal confusion. 'Good to see you again; how about a coffee?'

Bruce nodded and said, 'Thank you.'

'Irene, can we have two coffees, please?' Harry shouted.

'They won't be long,' came the reply from the outer office.

'Well now,' continued Harry, 'before we get down to business and go through the details of your patch, have you seen anything of Monaston yet?'

'Not a lot, apart from the town centre,' replied Bruce.

'The area,' said Harry, 'is not the most scenic inside the town but outside there is some attractive countryside. You must come over and see where I live. As for the people round here,' he continued, 'I think it's safe to say that you will find most of them pretty down-to-earth, plain-speaking and pragmatic. Many of them are suspicious of people from the Town Hall. They see us as pen-pushers and, to a degree, they're right; it's part of our job, isn't it, reports and all that? George Bernard Shaw held that all professions are conspirators against the laity. I think that is perhaps a little harsh or cynical but there's some truth in it.'

'Granted,' said Bruce.

'Above all,' Harry went on, 'the locals here appreciate plain English and you know as well as I do that psychologists' reports often appear to be a lot of gobbledegook to lay people. I'm all for plain English, in fact I'm a strong supporter of the PEC.'

'The Common Market?' Bruce asked.

'No, that's the EEC,' Harry replied with a smile, assuming Bruce was being deliberately humorous. He went on, 'The PEC is the Plain English Campaign and we certainly need one in this country. It's also my opinion that if you can't say what you want to say in plain English then you don't know what you are talking about. I'm a great believer in faith, hope and clarity. Anyway,' Harry continued, 'the locals here will trust you more if they've seen you. In short, home visits or domiciliaries, as we call them, are often more effective than conversations over the phone. In any case, most of them don't own phones so domiciliaries are essential.'

'I was used to home visits in my last job,' interjected Bruce as the secretary entered, armed with two coffees on a tray.

'Thank you Irene,' said Harry. 'Now regarding today, can I make a suggestion? The first day in a new job is usually a boring affair. You know, going round and shaking hands and meeting new people and all that. So, to make your first day colourful or at least one to remember,' here Harry raised his voice, 'why not throw yourself in at the deep end?'

Bruce's face betrayed a little anxiety, if not alarm.

'Don't worry,' added Harry with a smile. 'As usual I'm exaggerating. We've got two interesting cases at either end of the borough. They are as different as chalk and cheese but at least they will give you a taste of the variety we are capable of in Monaston.'

'First there is little Suzie Treadwell, out at Paradise Village, a case of spina bifida and severe hydrocephalus. The specialists tell us that she is allergic to the valve, the unidirectional valve which drains off the cerebral spinal fluid and so her head is very inflated. She is not a pretty sight and the home is deprived to say the least – two young parents, dad out of work and they also have twins younger than Suzie.'

'Twins!' exclaimed Bruce. 'One of my special interests; once wrote a paper on the subject entitled "Yours Twincerely". Do you know the most important thing which a mother of twins requires?'

Harry contemplated and then replied, 'A spin-dryer?'

'True,' replied Bruce. 'But I would also say a good husband to care for the one while she is dealing with the other. This came out of a discussion I once had at a Mother of Twins Group.'

'There's plenty of scope to set up such a group here,' Harry interjected. 'We psychologists all have our specialisms. You will soon find out that mine is the gifted and the talented and to counteract any criticism of elitism, I also have interests in dyslexia and Down's Syndrome. Some day I will let you know how those interests developed.

'Well, going back to Suzie Treadwell, as you know, Bruce, with the advent of the new 1971 Special Education Act, there is now no such thing as an ineducable child. The Education department has responsibility for all children. In the old days the likes of Suzie would have been left at home to vegetate and possibly, if she was lucky, she would have been admitted to a training centre run by the Health department. But from now on, all children, and that includes the severely handicapped, have the right to be taught by specialist qualified teachers, and for some children this may make all the difference. I appreciate that you can't make a silk purse out of a sow's ear but in some cases you may be able to make a hide wallet. Your job, Bruce, as you know, will be to get a full history of Suzie's case and to make recommendations as to what she needs educationally. You will find that Monaston is not badly prepared for the education of severely handicapped children. A lot of money has come from voluntary services and although many of the people around here are not well off, they are not ungenerous.'

'It should be an interesting visit,' Bruce said, 'but I shall need to come to you afterwards to discuss school placement and other facilities,' he added.

'That's what I'm here for,' replied Harry. 'Remember, two heads are better than one. I'm here to help if I can, and from time to time I shall pick your brains.'

'And now for case number two. This one is at the posh end of the borough – Hatley. It is an interesting case of a four-year-old named Electra Andrews. She was referred by one of our health visitors. The child is described as highly intelligent, verbally gifted and it would appear that she is bringing up her parents, rather than vice versa. Anyway, it would be useful if you could give her a full intelligence test among other things, and advise her parents how to deal with her. Have you got a map of Monaston and the district?'

'No, I was going to buy one,' replied Bruce.

'Have this one,' insisted Harry, passing Bruce a well-thumbed document. 'It's a bit out of date – I rarely use it. I know most of the roads around here like the back of my hand. Now,' he added, 'let me show you your own office. It's a bit smaller than mine but adequate. It's furnished with the bare necessities and you will no doubt add what you require as time goes on.'

Harry led Bruce to another room off the main office. Like Harry's own room, it was carpeted and furnished with a desk, chair, phone, two armchairs for informal interview purposes, a bookcase and a filing cabinet. A number of small attaché cases were on the desk. Bruce instantly recognised them as the containers of test material which were the tools or stock-in-trade of all educational psychologists.

'I feel spoilt,' said Bruce, recalling the time of his first appointment when he had to share both a room and test material with another psychologist.

'Well,' said Harry, 'we promised you your own accommodation and equipment at the time of the interview and now you have your own patch, so it's all yours. Remember, we psychologists have a lot of independence. We are regarded as consultants in our own right but we are employed by the local authority and so we are answerable to them to a degree. You're your own boss here, Bruce, but remember, if you need help I'm only a few doors away. I suggest that you get settled in. You may want to take a look at that pile of referrals,' said Harry, pointing to some documents piled in an in-tray on the desk, 'and if you have time you may consider popping out to see the two cases we've discussed to get a taste of Monaston. I've got an itinerary of four or five visits and I won't be back until about four thirty. By the way, for a midday snack there is a nice little café in the town square called the Crow's Nest. You'll understand the name when you get there.' With that, Harry rushed back to his own room, picked up two attaché cases containing test material and made a hurried exit.

After gathering his thoughts, Bruce sat quietly at his desk and examined the pile of papers in front of him. They were recent cases referred to the Schools Psychological Service that fell into his newly-created patch. There were about twelve altogether. Most appeared to be straightforward educational assessments but a few were a little more complicated, with social workers' and other reports attached to them. Not feeling in the mood for reading, and wishing to get a taste of his future working environment, Bruce spread his newly-acquired map of Monaston and district across his desk and worked out an itinerary for the day. He decided first to go to Paradise Village and see the case of spina bifida. The family were called Treadwell but they were not on the phone so it might be a wasted journey. However, after this, Bruce thought he might take a look at the local gypsy encampment which he had heard about, and possibly glean some interesting background information about the place. There was nothing like seeing something for yourself. He had noticed that there was at least one case involving a traveller's child in the pile of documents on his desk. Next he could drive across to the more salubrious area of Hatley and meet the infant prodigy, Electra Andrews. Who knows? thought Bruce. The district might be a good area to look for a house to live in.

Before leaving, Bruce rang Electra's parents and was surprised to find her father at home. Mr Andrews did shift work and so fortunately Bruce could meet both parents that day. The appointment was made on a flexible basis for around three o'clock. Having mapped out some directions and other relevant details on a piece of paper, Bruce picked up the relevant documents and test material and left his room. As he passed through the outer office, he noticed a well-dressed, elegant and attractive lady conversing with Irene, the secretary.

Seeing Bruce, Irene immediately seized the moment. 'Mr Whitford,' she called, 'may I introduce you to Mrs Craig, our educational welfare officer?'

'By all means,' replied Bruce.

'Please call me Sarah,' the lady added as she shook hands with Bruce.

'Mr Whitford is our new educational psychologist,' Irene continued. 'Dr Wilcox and Mr Whitford are now covering the area between them, and so you will be probably seeing a lot of each other in the future.'

'Hopefully,' said Bruce with a smile and, edging towards

the door he added, 'I hope you won't think I'm rude but I have two visits to make and I'm already behind schedule.'

'Good luck wherever they are,' added Sarah with a flashing smile as Bruce waved goodbye and disappeared through the office door.

As Bruce strode quickly down the corridor of the Town Hall, he thought to himself, there's a woman with the kind of features which cause men to walk into walls or lose attention whilst driving.

It took fifteen minutes to reach Paradise Village and as Bruce surveyed the district, he soon appreciated how its title was little indicative of its appearance. The address which Bruce sought was one of a group of small, dilapidated houses. Each had a portion of land in front of it and in some cases this was fenced off from its neighbours. Although the potential was there for front gardens, most of the land was uncultivated and covered in rocks and weeds. Some of the plots, like the Treadwells', contained what appeared to be a garden shed. The houses, along with others in the area, had originally been built for miners in the last century.

Bruce walked up what appeared to be a makeshift path of stone slabs and knocked at the door with his knuckles. The door was immediately opened by a young, dishevelled man clad in jeans and a dirty shirt. He wore no shoes and his socks were halfway off his feet.

'Good afternoon,' said Bruce with a forced air of confidence. A feeling of uncertainty and anxiety crept in as he beheld the spectacle before him. The outside door had opened straight into a room, the floor of which was stone and the furniture scant. A young lady, clad in a short skirt and blouse, sat on a fender seat by what appeared to be a burnt-out coal fire. She looked thin, gaunt and miserable. Although she was only in her early twenties, her face already betrayed signs of wrinkles. She held a cigarette in her right hand, which was covered in nicotine. Two young boys, who Bruce deduced were the twins Harry Wilcox had referred to, were playing with the cinders in the seemingly burnt-out fire. From time to time they squealed with delight when a few remaining sparks were located. Both children were ill-clad and bare-footed.

'I've come to see Suzie,' Bruce announced. 'I'm the educational psychologist from the Town Hall.'

'Come in,' said the young man. 'Dr Wilcox usually sees Suzie,' he added questioningly.

'Yes,' replied Bruce, 'but Monaston now has two educational psychologists, Dr Wilcox and myself, and so we have been able to split the area and hopefully we can now give a better or at least a quicker service.'

'What are you going to do with Suzie?' asked the young lady.

'You are her parents, I presume?' said Bruce.

'Yes, we are,' the young lady replied.

'Well,' Bruce continued, 'under the new law the local authority now has responsibility to care and provide for Suzie's education and general welfare. But before I make any recommendations, I need to ask you some questions about Suzie's abilities and then possibly do some little tests with her. Can I sit down somewhere and take some notes?'

The young man brought an old wooden chair from what appeared to be an adjoining scullery, which contained a washbasin, an old gas oven, some pots and pans and crockery. He placed the chair in the middle of the room and Bruce sat on it with care.

Before getting down to formalities, Bruce felt that a short, informal conversation would be helpful. He knew, as many members of his profession are aware, that small talk can be important for establishing a relationship. To some extent the description was a misnomer since small talk often lays the foundation for greater things. Those little conversations or remarks made before an interview can, in some cases, have more impact than any other.

After informing the Treadwells that this was his first working day in Monaston and learning how they themselves had spent their lives in the area, Bruce adopted a more formal approach. Taking a notebook from his document case, he proceeded to ask Suzie's parents details of her birth and early history and the difficulties of looking after a handicapped child with her kind of problems.

Suzie was now six years of age and was becoming quite heavy to carry around. She was doubly incontinent and needed frequent changing. Suzie's hydrocephalus was severe. She had the characteristic swollen and elongated head associated with the condition. The weight of her head meant that at times it was not easy to maintain an upright position. At the time of the interview, Suzie was lying prostrate on an old sofa and was trying to feed herself from a basin of cornflakes balanced on her chest. The possibility that such a posture might cause asphyxiation had gone unheeded by her young parents.

Bruce pulled his chair next to Suzie and asked her a few simple questions, to which she responded readily. The child smiled and appeared to enjoy the stimulation. Her eyes were alert and her verbal responses to the point. Bruce's interest grew, since Suzie's verbal ability surprised him. Children with her physical handicap often had serious brain damage and as a consequence low functional ability.

'What do you do with a ruler?' he asked.

'Measure of course,' replied Suzie smiling.

'In what way are a carrot and a potato the same? How are they alike?'

'You eat them and they both grow in the soil and they are both vegetables,' Suzie replied with a gleam in her eye.

In view of the child's severe physical handicap, together with the lack of suitable furniture in the house, Bruce was

Suzie was lying prostrate on an old sofa and was trying to feed herself from a basin of cornflakes balanced on her chest.

unable to administer tests which required constructional and manipulative skills. To perform these, Suzie would have required a table and a specially designed chair for the child to sit up in. However, from a brief sample of verbal items, Bruce's clinical experience taught him that this six-year-old child, despite all her physical and background problems, probably had at least a normal and possibly above-average, intellectual potential.

He lost little time in conveying these sentiments to the child's parents who showed obvious pleasure in the finding.

'I told you so,' said Mrs Treadwell to her husband. 'That girl has got more brains than us.'

'I shall arrange to see Suzie later and give her some more reliable tests,' said Bruce. 'She certainly has plenty of ability. Under the new law, that is the 1971 Special Education Act, the local education authority has the responsibility to provide a proper education for children who have disabilities like Suzie's. I shall recommend that to begin with she is offered a full-time place at a school or in a unit for children who have a physical handicap but who also have good intelligence.' Bruce emphasised the last point. 'A special bus or taxi will take Suzie there and bring her back every day. As well as being taught all the various subjects, we will recommend that she receives regular physiotherapy to help her to sit upright and move around. What do you think of that?'

'It sounds good,' replied Suzie's mum. 'She's never had any real schooling.'

'Are there any questions you would like to ask me?' continued Bruce.

'Well, there is one,' replied Mrs Treadwell.

'Yes?' said Bruce.

'I've got terrible toothache and I don't know what to do and my husband is out of work. Can you help?'

Bruce was a little perturbed at the nature of the question

but although dental hygiene and careers advice were somewhat outside his normal sphere of influence, he always tried to adopt a constructive approach in his work whatever the occasion.

'Leave the matter with me. I shall try to get something done as soon as possible,' he replied, and with that, he gathered up his equipment and bade farewell to the Treadwells.

As Bruce let himself out of the door, one of the twin boys still in his bare feet followed him. 'Watch that you don't get a cold or cut your feet,' Bruce cautioned the child.

The little boy seemed oblivious to the remarks and, with a gleam in his eye, he asked, 'Do you want to say goodbye to my granddad?'

'Where is he?' said Bruce.

'Here,' replied the child, simultaneously opening the door of the old shed in front of the house. Bruce was overwhelmed as he peered into the shed and beheld what could only be the fully-clothed corpse of an old man lying prostrate on a bench. 'He's going to Heaven on Thursday, my mum says,' shouted the little boy and, sporting a mischievous grin, he closed the door on the cadaver and ran back to the house.

Still taken aback and speechless, Bruce continued to the road where he found an elderly man and woman standing by his car. Leaning on a walking stick, the man, who was gaunt and gap-toothed, addressed Bruce. 'I see you've just paid your last respects to old Tom Treadwell,' he said. 'Dear old man, like many of us miners the black lung got him in the end.' The man who, with his wife, lived next door to the Treadwells was referring to the respiratory condition of pneumoconiosis which affected so many miners at that time.

'You've been to see little Suzie,' added the lady. 'Sad, isn't it? She's got water on the brain.' This was the common lay description of the medical condition known as hydrocephalus.

'Yes, I've been to see her,' Bruce answered politely.

'Those children are not fed on the right things, you know,' the old lady went on. 'We're the neighbours and I've been in there. One day I noticed that they had been eating custard for breakfast and in the middle of the day they have things like cornflakes.'

'Oh, do they?' replied Bruce as he recalled the plate of cereal balanced on Suzie's chest. 'Well, I must be off,' and with that he said, 'Cheerio,' jumped into his car and sped off toward his next destination.

It was a dull, mild and rather windless day. Bruce left his car window open. In the distance he could hear the clank of a fleet of coal trucks taking their cargo from the local mine to some unknown destination. Whilst driving, he picked up the rough map he had left on the passenger seat. This would guide him to his next visit via the gypsy encampment at Ruff Hollow. He had already had some interesting and not to say unusual experiences. What else could there be?

Ruff Hollow was situated on the southern border of Monaston, not far from its neighbouring town of Duckingford. Although named Ruff Hollow, the gypsy encampment was in fact situated on a rise or small hillock. The high ground was no doubt selected by the travellers for security against flooding.

As Bruce arrived at the encampment, he noted that the sky had become overcast and the whole atmosphere was unusually quiet. It was still mid-afternoon on a weekday in early September. Was a storm pending? The encampment was easily observable. It appeared to consist of a few battered cars, two lorries and a number of terrapin-like structures on blocks. Cats could be seen roaming around the vehicles and a goat with a long tether was munching the

A lady emerged from one of the terrapin-like structures, carrying a baby in one hand and a bucket in the other.

grass on a nearby verge. Bruce's curiosity was excited. He parked his car just off the road and walked a little closer to the site. A lady emerged from one of the terrapin-like structures, carrying a baby in one hand and a bucket in the other. She went to a nearby hydrant which was equipped with a turncock, and filled the bucket with water. As she waited for the bucket to fill, she turned and looked towards Bruce. He felt a little uncomfortable and pretended to look towards the road sign at the crossroads, as if trying to find out where he was. Just then another figure emerged from another mobile home. It appeared to be a lady in a long flowing dress, a colourful head garment and huge earrings. The lady herself was rather corpulent, all of fifteen stone, thought Bruce. She looked across at him and shouted, 'A storm is brewing!'

'Do you think so?' replied Bruce.

'I'm sure,' she continued, adding, 'what brings you to Ruff Hollow?'

'I'm new in these parts,' replied Bruce, 'getting to know the place.'

'You're from the Town Hall?' she said.

Rather perplexed, Bruce replied, 'Yes, how did you know?'

The fat lady grinned but didn't answer.

As Bruce turned to go, the woman called out, 'Would you like your hand read for a small piece of silver?'

Normally Bruce would have declined such an invitation. Being a good Catholic, he normally shunned anything to do with the Occult. However, on this occasion his curiosity got the better of him and since he harboured some interest in parapsychology he decided to take the risk and, accepting the invitation, followed the lady up the steps and through the door of her home.

Once inside, Bruce was ushered through a curtain and into a small compartment on the right. The only furniture in the compartment was a table and two chairs. On the table was what Bruce deduced to be a Ouija board and a set of tarot cards. He made it clear to the lady that he was in something of a hurry and only had a few minutes to spare.

'Fine,' said the lady. 'Sit here and show me your left hand.'

Bruce had a hazy idea that there was on the hand a lifeline, a sunline and a line of intuition, and that each was supposed to convey some significance.

'Do you work in an office?' she asked, holding Bruce's outstretched palm.

'Sort of,' replied Bruce, thinking that she already knew that he came from the Town Hall and that anyone could see that his hands did not betray the signs of manual work; she was not so clever.

'Does your name begin with B?' the lady went on.

'Yes,' replied Bruce, a little startled.

'And are you married with children?'

'Yes,' replied Bruce, again a little surprised since he did not wear a wedding ring. Was she guessing?

'Does your work involve children?'

'Yes,' he answered.

'And are you new in this area?'

This last comment was not so clever, thought Bruce, since he had already told her this.

'Now,' the lady went on, 'the important thing is... a warning. In the next year do not allow any relationship to upset your marriage. I see someone on the horizon.'

Bruce and his wife had been married for seven years. They were both devout Catholics and comments of this nature disturbed him a little. Sensing his reaction, the gypsy lady switched to comments on Bruce's early life. Again some of the statements surprised him, while others appeared less penetrating. The interview gradually came to a close. Bruce left some silver on the table – more than he originally intended and, bidding farewell to the lady, prepared to leave her home.

As he negotiated the steps outside, he became aware of a figure looming up before him. Below him, carrying a bucket of water, stood a mountain of a man with impressive jowls and a potato-like nose. He was waiting to enter the door which Bruce was vacating.

'Good afternoon,' said Bruce as the man stepped back and gave him a huge grin.

'Here comes trouble,' said the man to Bruce.

'Trouble?' Bruce answered, thinking that the remark was directed to the weather as a clap of thunder could be heard in the distance.

The man gesticulated towards the road where Bruce could just discern what appeared to be a group of motorcyclists coming over the brow of the hill.

Bruce had hardly reached his car when the group of five teenagers, clad in leather and goggles, drew up near the encampment and started hurling abuse, much of which appeared to be directed towards the man Bruce had just left. The man stared at them as they stood abreast of their bikes and broke into song:

> Jumbo Lee, Jumbo Lye, Jumbo Leo,
> Son of a bitch, he lives with a witch
> Down the Hollow!

The lines which they repeated and sang in unison were obviously well rehearsed. By this time the lady who had told Bruce's fortune had appeared at the door. One youth, a little more daring than the others, stood his bike up by the side of the road and walked towards the encampment, hurling abuse and insults as he did so.

The massive gypsy allowed him to come within ten

yards and then suddenly sprang to life. His speed was astonishing for a man of his stature. In a frenzied retreat, the youth half-slipped in the mud and Jumbo Lee, as he was known, grabbed one of his boots. Somehow the boy managed to escape by slipping out of the boot and throwing himself on the pillion of a waiting colleague as the group revved up their engines and made their retreat. Jumbo Lee waved the trophy of the boot towards Bruce, who had watched the whole incident with amazement. Bruce signified his admiration with a thumbs-up sign and waved goodbye. As he drove away he noticed that Jumbo Lee was moving the lone motorcycle, which had been abandoned by the youth, into the encampment. Serves the little beggar right, he thought.

Bruce's next destination was Hatley, which, along with the Mutley district, was possibly the nearest one could get to an upmarket suburb or stockbroker belt in Monaston. As he drove along, the thunder became more frequent and louder and was accompanied by lightning. Soon the rain began to fall. By the time Bruce entered Hatley, it was lashing down. The address he sought was Number 17, Coniston Drive, the home of Mr and Mrs Andrews and their daughter Electra. The house was one of a number of recently-constructed three-bedroom residences. They were attractively built, if similar in appearance. Bruce located the right number and noted that above the gate was the interesting name 'Whitsend'. He drew up outside the gate and, not having an umbrella or raincoat, contemplated how quickly he could get out of the car, lock it and reach the front door whilst still holding his test material. He could see what appeared to be the face of a small child pressed up against one of the front windows of the house. No doubt that was Electra, the subject of his visit.

For a brief spell the rain seemed to subside and Bruce made a dash for the front door. No sooner had he rung the

He could see what appeared to be the face of a small child pressed up against one of the front windows of the house.

bell than the door opened and there stood an alert and attractive, neatly-dressed four-year-old. She looked Bruce up and down and then commented in a manner far advanced for her tender years, 'You're the man who's come to test my ability. I'm afraid you won't find me very intelligent today. I'm suffering from the after-effects of chickenpox.'

From this brief statement Bruce deduced that he was in for something. 'Could I see your parents?' he enquired.

'Of course,' she replied in a mature tone. 'Come through – they are waiting for you in the lounge.'

Bruce walked through the hall to a well-furnished lounge at the back of the house. As he entered, the child's parents stood up and walked forward to greet him.

'You are Mr and Mrs Andrews?' asked Bruce.

'Yes,' replied the lady. 'Electra insisted on showing you in herself,' she said apologetically.

'Why not?' said Bruce.

After a short informal chat about the weather, he enquired whether it was possible for him to have a quiet place where he could do some tests with Electra.

'What about my study?' suggested Mr Andrews and added, 'There are a table and two chairs there.'

'Excellent,' replied Bruce, and with that Mr Andrews led him to the stairs.

'I'll take him to the room,' shouted Electra and, pushing her father to one side, led Bruce up the stairs to the smallest of three rooms. 'Here we are,' said Electra.

'Good,' replied Bruce. 'You sit here and I will sit there and we can put my tests and things on the table.'

For the next hour Bruce gave Electra a comprehensive battery of intelligence and scholastic tests. The little girl appeared to enjoy every moment of his individual attention as well as the challenge of the many interesting tasks. She beamed continuously as Bruce praised her responses. Electra literally romped through the tests. On a vocabulary measure, when asked what a thermometer was, she launched into the need for taking body temperature and how body heat could affect the workings of the various organs. On a test of conceptual thinking, she lost no time in abstracting the concept of a vegetable which grows in the soil, when asked in what way a potato and a carrot are alike. On non-verbal measures involving shapes and blocks, she perceived and matched up the required patterns with dexterity and speed.

When calculating her intelligence quotient, Bruce discovered that it went off the scale at over one hundred and fifty-five. Similarly when testing her reading and spelling ability, this alert little bundle of energy registered scores some five or six years ahead of her age level. When writing, her pencil manipulation was mature. She had already acquired what psychologists termed 'the dynamic tripod grip', in other words the apposition of thumb, index and middle finger employed in writing.

Bruce checked and rechecked Electra's various scores, consulted his tables of norms and confirmed that the child's abilities fell at the level educational psychologists described as 'very superior' or 'intellectually gifted'.

'Well,' said Bruce, packing his test material away and placing a piece of blank paper in front of Electra, 'I'm now going to give you a rest. I want you to stay here and draw me the very best picture of a lady that you have ever done in all your life and on the back of the paper I want you to write me a little story about the picture and, whilst you're doing it, I will go downstairs and tell your mummy and daddy what a clever girl you've been.'

Without looking up, Electra set about drawing a picture but as Bruce went to the door, she commented, 'I know why you don't want me to come down and listen to what you say. You think I would be embarrassed. In fact, I wouldn't be. I know I'm clever.'

Bruce looked a little perturbed and descended the stairs. Inside the lounge a cup of tea and biscuits were waiting for him. Only then did he realise that he had not eaten since breakfast.

'That's very welcome,' he said and, sitting down, he paused and looked at Mr and Mrs Andrews, who by this time were both sitting on the edge of their seats in apparent, patient expectation.

'Well,' Bruce commenced, thumbing the record sheets he had completed for Electra. 'You certainly have a clever girl up there. I've given her a complete intelligence test. Do you know anything about intelligence tests?' asked Bruce.

'Not really,' replied Mrs Andrews. 'Is that what you do when you take the eleven plus?'

'Not exactly,' replied Bruce. 'You see, there are only about three proper intelligence tests in the world. Each consists of a big case of things,' here Bruce pointed to his attaché cases of test materials, 'and they are quite complex instruments. They are standardised on all the various populations in different languages across the world. So you get the same tests in German, French, Spanish as well as English. What they do is measure abilities in all sorts of areas because, let's face it, you can show intelligence in a thousand and one different ways, can't you?'

Mr and Mrs Andrews nodded.

'But,' Bruce went on, 'there are two main ways, namely verbal,' he pointed to his mouth, 'that is, using words and what we call non-verbal, or visual-spatial and constructional tasks. Put it this way. A man can build your car engine or design the shape of your car. He's got what we call good mechanical, constructional or spatial intelligence. Right? But when he comes in to talk about what he's done or describe the process, or work out the bill, he may not be so clever at using words. Now I've given Electra a complete intelligence test and in both kinds of abilities, verbal and non-verbal, she went off the scale, that is, she hit the ceiling. In fact she achieved the highest possible score.'

'If I were a statistician,' Bruce went on, 'I would say that Electra's abilities are "one in a thousand". If I were a teacher, I might say "in a class of her own". If I were an astronomer,' he continued, smiling, 'I might say "out of this world". But I am an educational psychologist by trade, so I say that Electra's abilities come within the very superior range of intelligence or, if you like, at the intellectually-gifted level.'

Bruce paused as Mr and Mrs Andrews stared at him a little dumbfounded. He added, 'Did you realise that Electra has a very high ability?'

'We know she's bright,' said her father with a puzzled look.

'She's also very determined,' added Mrs Andrews. 'Last night she insisted that we went up to bed early whilst she watched the television on her own and if we didn't, she threatened a tantrum.'

Bruce could hardly believe his ears but he had come across this kind of case before. It was known as an 'infant autocrat' case, in which the child brings up her parents rather than the reverse. Child management counselling was required here as well as educational guidance. Where should he start?

'First, let's consider Electra's educational needs,' said Bruce. 'Have you thought about them? Remember, not only is she exceptionally intelligent but she is already reading and spelling at the ten-year-old level and she is only just four years old. Which school do you want her to go to?'

'I suppose that she would normally go to the local infants school down the road,' said Mr Andrews, 'but they won't admit them there until the term in which they are five, and unfortunately Electra's birthday is on 5th September.'

Bruce realised that here was another problem. Had Electra been born six days earlier, she would have been in the peer group above her normal one. So here was a child with a mental age of about eight years, who could read like a ten-year-old and who would in a year's time be placed in a large class of five-year-olds, most of whom might be unable to read or would be at the very earliest stages in developing literacy skills. A child with Electra's ability would need to be challenged and stretched, otherwise she would become vulnerable to under-achievement, frustration and behavioural difficulties.

'Does Electra ever play with other children of her own age?' asked Bruce.

'Not really,' replied Mrs Andrews. 'We paid for her to go to nursery when she was three but after two days she refused to go again because it was boring. She complained that all they did was play with water, sand and clay, and the stories which the teachers told were babyish.'

At this point Mr Andrews added, 'Electra gets on better with older children and with adults.'

'I'm not surprised,' said Bruce. 'How would you like me to get Electra admitted to school early and placed in a class where the children are on average a year older than she is? You see, the research into intellectually-gifted children suggests that, on the whole, they are also socially and emotionally more mature than their normal peer group and if you keep them in their age group, you are in fact pressurising them in another way. You are trying to make them average or level them down and this will make them become frustrated. I am not saying that acceleration or early promotion is always the best way to help these children, but it is one way. So we may think in these terms to begin with. What I shall do is to contact the head teacher of the local infants school and have a chat with her and discuss ways in which we can help Electra. I shall also send her a copy of my report, which will outline Electra's high abilities and her educational needs.'

The conversation at this point was unexpectedly interrupted by Electra, who had come downstairs, anxious to show Bruce the drawing she had done. Bruce examined the drawing with some amazement.

'So this is your picture of a lady?' he asked Electra and added, 'It's certainly an unusual lady. Her legs don't seem to be connected to her body and her eyes are a long way from her nose. Where are her arms?' he asked.

'It's a Picasso,' retorted Electra. 'Don't you know anything about Cubism?' she remarked with annoyance.

Bruce had difficulty suppressing a laugh as he complimented the child on her knowledge of Art. He then tried to pick up the thread of the conversation Electra had interrupted and, turning to her bemused parents, he drew their attention to a document which listed the titles of booklets and other references for helping gifted children.

'I would suggest that you purchase this one which is a practical guide for parents. With regard to managing Electra at home, I feel that you should not allow her to dominate you. Some parents, and indeed some teachers, are sometimes a bit fearful of clever children. What you have got to remember is that a child may have a very high intelligence but you have the wisdom, experience and greater maturity and you know, in the long run, most children like to know what to do and to be organised by adults. It makes them feel secure. I would suggest that you have confidence in yourself and remember you are in charge. You are also bigger and stronger than Electra,' he added with a grin.

As Bruce rose to leave, he could not help thinking that Mr and Mrs Andrews were not the most confident of individuals and that their little offspring would continue to rule the roost.

The storm had now subsided. It was almost 5 p.m. and

Bruce decided to drive back to his hotel, have a coffee and possibly some biscuits and write up the reports on the two cases he had seen that afternoon. He thought he could leave the section involving recommendations open until he had discussed these with Harry in the light of the local facilities available. By now Bruce was becoming familiar with the layout of Monaston and its environs. He did not take long to find his hotel, which was near the centre of the town. There was no car park attached to the hotel so he parked in a nearby public car park. He had been assured that it was quite safe to park there. Conveniently, Bruce saw a telephone box in a side road outside the car park. He could phone his wife, check on the family and give them the latest news.

As Bruce got out of his car, he recognised a lady making towards a nearby vehicle.

'We must stop meeting like this,' she shouted jokingly. It was Sarah Craig, the educational welfare officer whom Bruce had met earlier that morning in the education office.

'It is a bit risky,' Bruce replied with a smile. 'Is your day over?'

'Not yet,' Sarah answered. 'I often do home visits at night when you can catch both parents home from work. Some of the places I visit are so questionable that I could do with a chaperon!'

'Well, I'm always here,' Bruce added with a twinkle in his eye and by this time he had walked up to Sarah's car.

'Do you know Monaston very well?' enquired Sarah.

'I'm getting to know it,' replied Bruce, adding, 'Today I've visited Paradise Village, Ruff Hollow and Hatley, so you could say that I now have some acquaintance with the area.'

'You've done well for one day,' said Sarah.

There was a slight lull in the conversation.

Bruce quickly broke the silence. 'Well I must now find a

phone box and ring home and check on the family.'

'There's one over there,' Sarah suggested, pointing to the far edge of the parking area.

'Thanks,' said Bruce and bidding farewell he made his way towards the telephone box. He was soon chatting away with Marie, his wife, and hearing about his eldest child's first day back at school. Josephine, known as Josie, had fallen in the playground and chipped one of her teeth. Fortunately, it was the first dentition. Marie had been called into the school and took Josie straight to the dentist.

'And what kind of day have you had?' Marie asked.

Bruce paused, reflecting on the many incidents and varied characters, as well as the inclement weather, he had encountered on his first working day in Monaston.

'Well,' he said, 'it is certainly different to working in the big town but I think I'm going to like it.'

'Have you met anyone nice?' continued Marie.

'Yes, there are some nice people here,' Bruce replied slowly and thoughtfully, simultaneously looking through the glass door of the phone box where he saw Sarah Craig waving to him as she drove through a nearby exit of the car park. He attempted to wave back whilst continuing the conversation. 'There appears to be a lot of driving in this job,' he informed Marie.

'Well, be careful, dear,' she warned. 'Better late in this world than early in the next.'

Chapter Three
Riddler on the Roof

It was Bruce's second day in Monaston. He had arranged to see Harry in the office first thing in the morning in order to discuss ways of helping the two cases he had seen the day before.

'Two heads are better than one,' Harry had said, and from time to time he expected to seek advice from Bruce, and Bruce would always be welcome to do the same from him. More importantly today in view of Bruce's present lack of knowledge of Monaston and district, it would be necessary to consult Harry with regard to the local facilities for special education.

Harry was already in his office when Bruce arrived.

'Come in,' he shouted, as Bruce knocked on the door. 'How did the rest of your day go?' he enquired, hardly looking up from his desk, which was as ever immersed in documents.

'Fine,' said Bruce.

'So you've solved the problems?'

'Not exactly,' replied Bruce. 'First I went to the Treadwells' to see Suzie – the home is a bit deprived isn't it?'

'Most of our cases are sad,' replied Harry. 'Some are bad and a fair number are mad. Did you ever see the film *Knock on Any Door* starring Humphrey Bogart? Behind many doors are stories, sometimes of great sadness.'

'I know what you mean,' replied Bruce, 'and I should

imagine that there are plenty of examples in Paradise Village.'

'This part of the county has been a priority area for the last three years,' Harry went on, 'but nothing much has changed. Unemployment, stone floors and decaying housing are a way of life in some parts. I could take you to at least one dwelling where a child's bed is nothing more then a pile of rags in the corner. George Bernard Shaw said that he didn't believe in circumstances as an excuse for failure, but when I see the backgrounds of some of the children here, I think they have every excuse.'

'I understand that under the new law,' Bruce was referring to the 1971 Special Education Act, 'no child is deemed ineducable, so we have an obligation to arrange education for Suzie as soon as possible. She is already over statutory school age.'

'Correct,' replied Harry.

'My feeling is,' Bruce continued, 'that her intellectual potential is at least normal, so we need a placement which caters for a child of normal intelligence who at present is non-ambulant or chair-bound. Have we a school for physically-handicapped children?'

'Of course,' said Harry, 'the Wimbourne Fields School for PH children. It's a county school about five miles outside the borough. So we ought to get Sarah in; she is the education welfare officer for that area. But first it may be useful to arrange for a full diagnostic assessment at the Mutley Child Development Centre.'

'Mutley?' asked Bruce.

'Yes, the Mutley Clinic,' replied Harry. 'It's one of these new institutions set up to encourage interdisciplinary co-operation. Professionals work together in a spirit of collaborative independence.' Harry emphasised the last phrase with his tongue in his cheek. 'We all pool our knowledge and, hopefully, the results help the children.

Oh, another important point is that parents are involved and their wishes must be considered. No matter what we professionals think, we can't bully parents into accepting our ideas – at least that's the spirit of the new approach. It doesn't always work in practice, of course.'

Harry continued, 'The three to six-year-olds who are difficult to place can spend the mornings at the clinic with their mothers and fathers for a fortnight if they wish. They are given transport if necessary. For most of the time, trained nursery nurses look after them, and from time to time the professionals visit the clinic and do their assessments. These people include physiotherapists, speech therapists, school doctors, paediatricians, health visitors, clinical psychologists and us – in fact, the whole panoply. Sometimes the dietician from the local hospital even takes part. We try to stagger our visits because of the shortage of rooms. The educational psychologists usually visit on Tuesdays or Thursdays. At the beginning of each fortnight we are sent a list of half a dozen or so names and addresses. Most of the cases are pre-school children aged between three and five years old. You can look down the list and if any one of the names falls in your patch, it's your job to arrange to see the child, make an assessment of the child's educational needs and have the written report ready by conference day, which takes place on the last Friday afternoon of each fortnight. Generally, it works like clockwork. Our secretaries know that the reports have to be ready by conference day and so they make sure that they are. So, what do you think, shall we put Suzie in for a diagnostic session at Mutley?'

'Sounds good to me,' replied Bruce, and then he added, 'By the way, there are two other points about the family. Mr Treadwell is out of work and Mrs Treadwell was complaining of toothache while I was there. She seemed quite helpless and didn't know who the nearest dentist was or how to get there. Can we help?'

'Oh,' replied Harry, and then with a little hesitation added, 'the answer is Delia Berry, in fact you will soon discover that Delia is the answer for a lot of things. She is a qualified senior psychiatric social worker and in fact the only one that the Education department here employs. There is a move to place all social workers under the new Social Services department but our local education authority recognises the advantage of employing their own social worker and in this case that's Delia Berry.

'Delia is married to Canon Berry. He is on the Education Committee and administers the Church of England schools in this region. You will find that Delia is a very energetic individual who has endless contacts, thrives on work and knows all the loopholes for getting around problems. Every so often she does something which annoys someone in authority and they leave off speaking to her for a while. But it makes no difference to Delia – it's like water off a duck's back – out of the blue, she will get on the phone to the person in question or breeze into his or her office as if nothing has happened and hey presto! – all is forgotten.

'I suggest you tell Delia about the problems of the Treadwells. Emphasise the need for a dental appointment and the fact that Mr Treadwell is out of work – she will do something about it. When she has done it, tell her what a wonderful woman she is – we all like praise, don't we? Delia thrives on work and praise.'

'I will try to remember that,' said Bruce. 'By the way, before I visited the little genius at Hatley, I had a look at the gypsy encampment at Ruff Hollow and had an interesting experience.'

'Don't tell me,' interrupted Harry, 'Crystal Lee read your palm.'

'Well, yes,' replied Bruce, a little disconcerted. 'Is there anything wrong with that?'

'Not really,' said Harry, 'apart from the fact that she is nearly always right. One of our local residents crossed her when she visited her house on one occasion and she swore that there would be a fatality in the family in the near future. Within three days a child in the family was killed by a car. Some regard Crystal as more of a witch than a fortune teller. Anyway, beware!' exclaimed Harry with a smile on his lips.

'I shall,' Bruce grinned, but underneath he was reflecting on the warning the gypsy had given him.

Bruce also told Harry about the motorbike incident and the taunting song concerning Jumbo Lee.

'I've heard it before,' replied Harry, 'and I wouldn't be surprised if some of those motorbikes were stolen and were being ridden by some of our local delinquents who should have been at school.'

'Well, let's talk about the young superbrain, Electra,' said Harry. 'What was the family like?'

'Middle class suburbia, seemed to be quite well-off, judging by the house and its contents,' replied Bruce. 'But the child could be a problem in school. She went off the top of the scale of an intelligence test, and is already reading and spelling like a ten-year-old – she is only four. She also tends to "rule" her parents. They do exactly as she orders them.'

'I see,' chipped in Harry, 'we have an intellectually-gifted child who is also an *enfant terrible*. So what do you propose we do with her?'

'Well, the best form of acceleration is early admission into school, is it not?' said Bruce. 'And in Electra's case, this would not be such a dramatic step as she is a September birth and as such, is already among the eldest in her age group.'

Harry was pondering. 'Well, the idea is good. What we

need in this country is the ruthless promotion of talent. There's only one problem and that's the head teacher of the local school, Miss Lister. She's rather set in her views. Once you approach her on the subject, she will probably lecture you on failing to consider that a child's social and emotional development must also be taken into account. So what you do next is point out that Electra is known to relate better to older children and adults anyway, and all the research we have in this area, namely Terman's genetic studies of genius, suggests that gifted children tend to be more emotionally and socially mature than their peers on the whole. There is nothing wrong with acceleration as long as it's done with conviction and tempered with flexibility and humanity. If you don't make headway then perhaps you could approach Mrs Green, who runs the local C of E school downtown and not so far from Hatley.'

'Thanks for the information,' said Bruce, taking notes as he listened.

'Yes,' muttered Harry and added in a lowered tone, 'Grace Green never says no to anyone, not even the caretaker, so they say, her private life is the subject of much innuendo.'

Bruce looked a little perplexed.

'Well,' said Harry, 'I'm fairly flexible in the next hour. What about going down to Mutley right now? See what you think of the place. We also have a unit for maladjusted children down there run by Doris Dicker.' Harry paused, reflected and added, 'She's a rather unorthodox lady.'

Within fifteen minutes Bruce and Harry had arrived in the car park of the Mutley Child Development Centre. The centre was not the quietest of places on that Tuesday morning. The office was a hive of activity with the phone in constant use. Parents were sitting and chatting in the reception area and the noise of young children could be heard whenever the door of the play area, which adjoined

She rides a bicycle to work and wears luminous stockings for safety.

the office, was opened.

Having introduced Bruce to the secretarial staff with some uncertainty, not to say trepidation in his voice, Harry suggested that they went down the corridor to take a quick look at the adjustment unit which Doris Dicker was in charge of.

'You will probably find Doris somewhat abrupt and maybe a little rude,' warned Harry. 'Her appearance is also unusual. She rides a bicycle to work and wears luminous stockings for safety. The staff comment that they look "ri*dicker*lous", a play "upun" words of course,' Harry went on. 'She lives in a house called "The Dickerage". Doris is very unorthodox and to some extent that is why we appointed her. The famous cosmologist, Fred Hoyle, believes that if a problem has an orthodox solution, the scientific community would have already found it, so he looks for the unorthodox solution, and that is exactly what we did when we appointed Doris Dicker. Orthodox treatment has not worked with most of the problem children in this unit and so we turned to the other extreme – there's no one more unorthodox than Dicker.'

'Incidentally,' Harry went on, 'before I introduce you I think you ought to know that in Doris's eyes I am not exactly flavour of the month. In fact some would say I am her *bête noire* or pet aversion.'

'Ah,' said Bruce knowingly, recalling the frequent differences in opinion he had experienced over the years among teachers. 'Your professional judgements have clashed, right? You are on different sides of the fence?'

'You could put it that way,' replied Harry, adding 'especially at weekends.'

Bruce looked confused.

'I will give you the details later,' said Harry with a twinkle in his eye, and with that he knocked tentatively on the door of the unit.

After about half a minute, the door swung open and a middle-aged lady with straight hair and worn features appeared. She wore a plain jumper and skirt with bright yellow stockings. She glared straight at Harry and said, 'Yes?'

Harry, whose composure had hitherto been a little apprehensive, suddenly straightened up and with a broad beam on his face, carefully modulating his voice, expostulated, 'Hello Doris, I've brought my new colleague, Bruce Whitford, to meet you. As, no doubt, you will be working together a lot in the near future, I thought you might like to meet Bruce now whilst he is at the clinic.'

Doris, who rather resembled the actress Patricia Hayes, with her haystack-like hair, in the role of Edna the Inebriate Woman, looked Bruce up and down very much as a farmer would have eyed a specimen of cattle at a market and then, after due thought, replied, 'Why not, Bruce? Come in.'

Harry, anticipating that the invitation would not extend to him, quickly interjected, 'Well Doris, I will leave Bruce in your safe hands,' and with that, he beat a hasty retreat.

Hardly had Bruce entered the unit when Doris was confronted by a deputation of three young lads complaining that a certain pupil by the name of Andrew Pester had completely ruined their papier mâché model of a horse.

'Pester,' yelled Doris, 'if you can't learn to behave yourself you will never get back to normal school.' Doris never minced her words. Tact was irrelevant to her management of children with behavioural disorders. Yet despite her forthright, abrupt and often harsh manner, Doris was well known to relate better to animals and problem children than to her fellow adults. She seemed to have an instinctive empathy with both groups and they also with her. Such empathy was no doubt born from a tough childhood in the depression of the 1930s and wartime London. She had been orphaned when her mother was killed in the Blitz and her father died in North Africa within a month. Having had the cards stacked against her in the early years, she had developed into a natural champion of the underdog. Doris had little respect for authority and even less for celebrities. However, she took a great deal of interest in local tramps, the elderly and incapacitated people. If the best index of a person's character is in the manner in which they treat those who can't fight back or do you any good, then Doris Dicker was a paragon.

Ever the opportunist and a person of considerable resourcefulness, Doris saw in the visit of Bruce the chance to help discipline her motley band of young deviants.

'Do you know who this gentleman is?' she asked in a lowered voice, staring from one child to another.

There was a pause and then Severn Duffy, a child from a notorious Monaston family who had been named Severn because he was the seventh child of parents who claimed they had run out of names, volunteered, 'He came with Dr Wilcox so he must be a shrink.'

Doris appeared completely unperturbed by the reply. Her weather-beaten face remained expressionless and, staring hard at Severn, she paused deliberately and replied, 'He is not a shrink, he is a man from the education office who has come to inspect your work. After he has inspected it, he is going to report back to the people in the education office whether he thinks it is good or bad, and whether he thinks any of you should be sent away.'

Bruce's posture stiffened. He realised that in the presence of such a forceful character as Doris it was safer to assume the role she had instantly created for him.

'So,' continued Doris, again slowly and deliberately, 'everyone sit at your desks, take out your work and place it on top of the desk ready for inspection.'

The group of six boys and three girls complied immediately.

As Bruce surveyed the scene, he could not help but feel that this was a latter day Dotheboys Hall with a difference.

'Right,' ejaculated Doris, 'we will start with Freddie Murphy. Freddie is here because he didn't like going to school. He is what the psychologists call a "school phobic" aren't you Freddie?'

Freddie was left in no uncertain terms as to what he was.

'Yes, Miss Dicker,' he replied.

'But,' continued Miss Dicker, 'Freddie likes it here and he is never absent from the unit. Isn't that true, Freddie?'

'Yes, Miss Dicker.'

'And why are you always here?' Doris lowered her voice and Freddie looked uncomfortable. 'I'll tell you why,' she went on. 'Because if you dare to stay away, I shall come personally to your house and drag you here,' she yelled with a half smile on her lips. The whole group, including Freddie, appeared to enjoy the joke, although they all knew that it contained some truth.

Doris ran a very tight ship and this extended to her teaching methods as well as her discipline.

'Mr Whitford is now going to inspect your work,' she continued, 'so put your writing book on top and your arithmetic book underneath and at the bottom your project book.' Doris then proceeded to guide Bruce from desk to desk of her nine pupils. At each stop she gave an account of the child's background, supposedly in an undertone so the child could not hear, but in reality the child concerned in each case would not have found it too difficult to comprehend the various statements made. Many of the statements were hardly a way to promote the dignity of a child.

After Freddie Murphy, the next pupil to be scrutinised was Alison Maypole, a smiling blue-eyed lass who had once been placed in a residential school for maladjusted girls in the London area. Alison had in fact set fire to the school and burnt it down. The local authority was experiencing difficulty in finding an alternative placement for Alison and so Miss Dicker had agreed to allow her to join the adjustment unit.

'Comes from a very deprived background in the Sockton area,' said Doris. 'She had a lot of bad habits which teachers and parents could not control. One of them was biting the heads off goldfish.'

Continuing in her lowered tone which was still audible halfway across the classroom, Doris came to Derek Waller, the eldest of three boys. 'Another unfortunate case,' she said. 'The mother is a schizophrenic and recently had a fixation that her children suffered from constipation and as a result she fed them on Ex-Lax and various diuretics. The specialist never had a clue what was happening. Dr Wilcox even wrote to ERIC.'

'Eric?' exclaimed Bruce questioningly.

'Yes, Eric,' repeated Doris. 'Haven't you heard of the organisation ERIC?' she said with affected surprise, obviously enjoying the apparent ignorance of a specialist. 'ERIC stands for Enuresis Resource and Information Centre. They can be useful but on this occasion were totally irrelevant. I discovered the root of the problem from the child himself when he told me he and his brothers were given lots of this new kind of chocolate called Ex-Lax. It's amazing what you can learn from the children themselves, if only people will talk and listen to them.'

At that moment one of the children let out a noise which could only resemble the bark of a dog.

'Just ignore him,' Doris muttered. 'That's Peter Dibble. Fortunately his bark's worse than his bite, he never shouts or screams, just barks. Flash Harry' – Bruce deduced that Doris was referring to Harry Wilcox – 'calls it Tourette's Syndrome. I call it Mad Dog Disease.'

'Oh yes,' interjected Bruce, 'it's an interesting condition, Tourette's Syndrome, a sort of compulsive obsessive disorder, or a tic. Some children grunt, some squeak, others blink or even swear and Peter, it seems, barks.'

'Yes,' replied Doris, not over-impressed with Bruce's knowledge of the condition. 'Ah! Michael Crump,' she continued, thumbing through the next child's books. 'Michael is trying. In fact,' she went on, 'you could say he's very trying,' and then in her customary loud whisper, she explained how this child had a very short 'fuse'.

'Yes, I understand, a poor frustration tolerance,' added Bruce knowingly.

'That's it,' said Doris. 'If anything upsets him, he goes berserk and then begins to undress himself. The first thing which comes off are his glasses and he flings them across the room. The secret is to get Michael in a half nelson or a body lock before he gets to his underwear and that is not always easy.'

'You've got to be an expert in wrestling then,' Bruce commented.

'Which is what I am,' replied Doris. 'Didn't you learn that from Dr Wilcox?'

'No, should I have?' Bruce said questioningly, and added, 'I only arrived in Monaston two days ago.'

'Let me put you in the picture,' Doris went on. 'Wednesday night is wrestling night over in Duckingford Town Hall.' Duckingford was the sister town immediately attached to Monaston; in fact they were so contiguous that they were often lumped together as one. 'I never miss it and neither does Flash Harry. But we usually support opposite opponents. He is a "Golden Terror" supporter whereas I side with Sailor Nick who is smaller but a much better wrestler. But that's only part of the story. Harry Wilcox and I are again on opposite sides at weekends. Hasn't he told you that he's a member of the local hunt?'

'No,' exclaimed Bruce with surprise, as further dimensions of Harry's colourful personality emerged.

'His Nibs, Dr Wilcox, is one of the Masters of the Hunt. Would you believe it?' Doris continued in a half sneer. 'And I,' she paused, 'am a sab.'

'A sab?' asked Bruce.

'Yes, a sab,' she went on, 'a hunt saboteur. We don't believe in cruel sports such as fox-hunting. It's cruel, it's childish and it's against nature.' Doris's face showed a flush of anger. 'We will stop it in the end. I've even lobbied MPs on the subject. One day we will win. But at present we are not doing so badly by making life awkward for them. Anyway, you will, no doubt, hear the other side from His Nibs.'

An extraordinary woman, thought Bruce. On the one hand Doris Dicker supported men brutalising themselves in the ring, yet on the other hand she objected to them hunting an inveterate and often bloodthirsty chicken and rabbit killer.

At that moment Bruce realised the coincidental significance of his earlier statement to Harry about being on the other side of the fence. In the context of a fox-hunt, Doris and Harry would literally be on different sides of the fence. Harry must certainly have appreciated the humour behind Bruce's artless statement.

Doris appeared to be in an informative mood and Bruce, ever inquisitive, took advantage of the situation to learn about those he was working with. 'You weren't raised in these parts?' he asked Doris, referring to her obvious south-east accent.

'No, I'm a Londoner through and through,' she replied, 'brought up in the East End. Lost both parents in the war. I've been an orphan with few relatives for most of my life.'

'And what about Harry Wilcox? Does he come from this area?' Bruce enquired.

'Well,' retorted Doris, 'no one is sure where he comes from. He lives in a cottage up on the Earl of Beersford's estate at Hackford Hall. It has been suggested that he could be one of Old Beery's offspring.' Doris hesitated to add the word 'illegitimate'. 'We know Harry went to public school; he certainly gives that impression when he mingles with the yobs in the hunt and all that. I suppose Flash Harry is a bit of an institution around here. Some say he punches above his weight when it comes to education and other matters.'

The character of Harry Wilcox continued to become ever more colourful in Bruce's mind. Not only did his new colleague appear flamboyant but he also assumed an air of mystery with his possible aristocratic connection.

Bruce felt he had learnt enough for one day. Time was pressing. He needed to snatch some lunch and motor out to an afternoon case in Barton Hope, a neighbouring village. He thanked Doris for showing him round, shook hands, bade farewell to the children in the unit and went to find Harry, who he hoped would drop him back at the Town Hall car park. On arriving at the reception, however, Bruce discovered that this was not to be. Shortly after leaving Bruce with Doris Dicker, Harry had been summoned to the phone.

'Mrs Berry wants to speak to you urgently,' the secretary had called to him.

'Hello, Delia, how are you?' enquired Harry, picking up the phone and adding, 'I've just been extolling your virtues to our new EP.'

'Thanks,' replied Delia. 'I'm looking forward to meeting him but there's no time at the moment, Harry. This is urgent. Does the name Lewis Walker ring a bell?'

Harry paused and quickly reflected. 'Isn't he the dyslexic up at Alderman Brown's School, who complains of being bullied?'

'Exactly,' Delia retorted, 'and right now he's sitting on the roof of his house, threatening to jump off if he is made to go back to school.'

Harry paused again. He realised that the boy's predicament was probably a cry for help, but threats of suicide should always be taken seriously – the number of suicides among teenagers had increased in recent years.

'Life is not like a cricket match. You only get one innings. So how can I help?' said Harry. 'This seems to be a job for the fire brigade, not an EP.'

'Believe me, Harry,' Delia pleaded, 'the situation is extremely sensitive, desperate in fact. The appearance of the fire brigade could send him over the top. Lewis's mother claims that you're the only one he has ever related to or trusted. If anyone can talk him down, it's you.'

'I feel flattered,' replied Harry, 'but not very confident. Okay, I'll do my best. Give me fifteen minutes.' Harry collected his belongings, briefly explained the situation to the secretary, asked her to apologise to Bruce and hurried to the car park.

Within a quarter of an hour, Harry was outside the Walkers' house, where by this time a small crowd had gathered. He was greeted by Delia Berry who had warned him that the situation was nearly explosive. He looked up to see the figure of a boy sitting on the rim of the roof in a foetal posture. Nearby on a chimney stack, the family's ginger cat had joined the child, having chosen an easier ascent via a lean-to at the back of the house. Harry vaguely recognised the child as Lewis Walker, whom he had interviewed some two weeks before. The child had been suffering from serious spelling and reading problems (sometimes referred to as dyslexia) and had developed a complex about it. The situation had come to a head on one occasion when he had been made to read aloud in front of the class, and this had been followed by ridicule and verbal bullying on the part of the other children. Nor had Lewis's teacher been particularly helpful. Whilst he condescendingly listened to Harry's explanation of the boy's problems,

He looked up to see the figure of a boy sitting on the rim of the roof in a foetal posture.

one felt that the teacher's whole attitude, like many professionals at the time, was sceptical about the very existence of dyslexia. The result had been that Lewis had developed an increasingly negative attitude towards school and was now refusing to go altogether.

On seeing Harry, Mrs Walker ran forward and pleaded, 'Dr Wilcox, please help to get Lewis down. I'm sure he will listen to you.'

'How did he get up there?' enquired Harry.

'Through the skylight,' replied Mrs Walker, indicating a small window which opened flush with the roof. Harry realised that little could be achieved by shouting to the boy from the road. What was required was closer physical proximity without actually getting on to the roof.

'Would it be possible for me to poke my head through the skylight?' Harry asked.

'Yes, if you don't mind going up into the loft. It's a bit dusty up there,' said Mrs Walker.

Harry quickly suggested to Delia that it would be helpful if she encouraged the crowd to disperse, and then set off into the house.

Within minutes he had ascended into the loft via a stepladder and was carefully groping toward the small window in the roof. He pushed it open carefully and managed to squeeze his head through the aperture, twisting himself into a position which enabled him to see the boy, who was crouching on the rim of the roof.

'Hello, Lewis,' he exclaimed, 'how are you feeling?'

'I'm cold and I want a riddle,' replied the boy and added, 'I can't do it in front of everyone.'

Harry reflected quickly. So that was the reason for the child's foetal position, not, as some would have interpreted it, an unconscious desire to return to the womb.

Appreciating Lewis's predicament, Harry suggested, 'Why not take off your coat, put it over your knees and do it underneath?' He added, 'It would be like rain going down the roof. I'll pop inside whilst you do it.' Harry discreetly closed the window and waited a few minutes, during which time the child, with some difficulty, managed to relieve himself. When Harry reopened the window the boy appeared less agitated. Harry realised that diversionary tactics might be helpful to defuse the situation.

'Can I tell you something, Lewis?' he said.

'What?' replied the boy.

'My grandfather,' Harry continued, 'was used as a spy in the First World War. Just like you, he was very nimble, he could climb anywhere. He was also a good artist and they used to make him climb trees and then survey the landscape and plot out where the enemy positions were. Sometimes he would make a sketch whilst up in the tree and at other times he would remember the picture and draw the plan when he got down.'

'I'm not going back to school,' said Lewis.

'Can you trust me?' replied Harry.

The boy appeared to nod.

'I will arrange for you to go somewhere better, and it won't be back to that school. Is that agreed?' asked Harry.

Lewis pondered, but before he could reply, Harry interrupted. 'Before you come through this window, I want you to do me a favour. This is, in fact, a memory test. I want you to look across, beyond the houses, to the countryside over there,' Harry gesticulated with his hand, 'and try to remember exactly what you can see. I will give you half a minute.' Lewis surveyed the countryside beyond the town whilst Harry looked at the second hand of his watch. After thirty seconds he said, 'Now Lewis, don't look over there again but just look at me down here and see how easily you can climb down and get through the window. Remember, I've promised you that you are not going back to that school.'

Harry held his breath. Would his diversionary plan work? Was it too obvious for a teenager? If it was, perhaps Lewis still wanted an excuse to extricate himself from such a difficult position. Slowly but surely the boy began to move. He was wearing trainers which gave him a good grip on the tiles. Harry held the vent open as Lewis lowered himself through and into the loft.

A few minutes later, Lewis's parents, joined by Delia Berry and Harry Wilcox, were having a discussion and coffee around the kitchen table. Mr Walker, Lewis's father, had been informed of the incident, and had been released from his post as a surface worker at the local mine. Like his wife he appeared confused but visibly relieved that no harm had come to the child. At Harry's suggestion, Lewis had gone to his bedroom and was producing a sketch from memory of the landscape he had seen from the roof of the house.

'You know what started all this?' said Mrs Walker. 'It's this,' she added, placing an opened exercise book on the table and pointing to a page of Lewis's writing which had a red line struck through it and the comment 'Write out every spelling mistake twenty times' at the bottom. 'Lewis spent a long time doing that for his homework two evenings ago,' continued Mrs Walker. 'I know he did because he did it on this table and we weren't allowed to make any noise or have the television on. That's the result of the boy's efforts.'

Both Delia and Harry perused the work with interest.

'I think it's a good effort,' remarked Harry and added, 'Plenty of people make spelling mistakes.'

'I'm not much of a speller myself,' added Delia.

'If Lewis doesn't want to go back to that school, he's not going back,' maintained Mr Walker.

'Exactly,' agreed Harry. 'The headmaster at Alderman Brown's is a good one and I get on well with him, but unfortunately there are still many teachers who don't understand or won't accept dyslexia. So we must give Lewis a fresh start. What do you think, Mrs Berry?' said Harry, turning to Delia.

'What about Hatley High? It's a nice school and they are about to set up a dyslexic unit there,' Delia replied.

'That thought was going through my head,' replied Harry. 'I wonder if Lewis has finished his sketch yet. Could you ask him to join us, Mrs Walker?'

Mrs Walker went out of the room and called for Lewis. Within seconds the boy had joined the group with his sketch of the landscape.

'Remarkable,' said Harry, examining the child's work. 'Lewis,' he added, 'this is brilliant. You've got what we psychologists call an excellent spatial memory.'

'He's always been good at art,' said Mrs Walker beaming.

'You are very lucky, Lewis, to have such an ability,' said Harry. 'I love art but I can't draw a teapot myself. Did you know that people who are good at art or technical drawing or constructing things are often bad spellers? Einstein was one, Leonardo da Vinci, the greatest engineer who ever lived, was another. What you must understand is that we are talking about a brain difference. Some people's brains are made in such a way that they are good spellers but poor artists and others are good artists and poor spellers. Do you understand what I mean, Lewis?' The boy nodded.

'Well,' continued Harry, 'think about what you are good at and don't worry so much about what you are bad at. Now, Lewis, while you have been doing this drawing for us, we have come up with some ideas. One is that we are going to try to get you transferred to Hatley High School where you can make a fresh start and, above all, they have a special unit there which you can attend from time to time to be helped with your spelling and reading. What do you think of that?'

Lewis paused and then quietly replied, 'Sounds okay.'

'Right,' said Harry, standing up. 'So my next step is to try to arrange for Lewis to go to Hatley.'

Having been informed that Dr Wilcox had had to depart on urgent business from Mutley Clinic, Bruce wondered how he would return to the Town Hall.

'Don't worry,' said the secretary, smiling. 'We've arranged your transport back to the education office. Sarah is going to take you.'

Bruce turned around and beheld Sarah Craig, the attractive education welfare officer whom he had already met the day before and who was visiting the clinic to counsel some parents on transport arrangements for their children who were to attend a local special school in the near future. She seems to be everywhere, mused Bruce to himself, especially when I need help.

'I'm ready when you are,' said Sarah.

'It's jolly good of you to do this for me,' replied Bruce.

'I've got to go back to the office anyway,' she said and with that, they left the clinic and walked to the car park.

Once on the way, conversation seemed to flow easily. 'So where are you going this afternoon?' asked Sarah.

'I've got a behavioural problem case in Barton Hope,' said Bruce, 'my first visit to the village.'

'And it won't be your last,' retorted Sarah. 'There are plenty of problems up there.' She appeared to speak with experience and authority.

Once they arrived in the car park neither Bruce nor Sarah appeared to be in any rush to get out of the car. They seemed to be enjoying each other's company and so the conversation continued and soon got into the realm of more personal matters. Bruce talked enthusiastically about his own family. His wife was a qualified nurse from Yorkshire who was no longer employed as such, having her work cut out with looking after three small children, two of whom were still at pre-school age.

'Marie is now a domestic engineer,' he said and went on to relate how he had already taught his two eldest children the basics of reading.

'All the research shows that children who can read when they go to school are ahead at eleven,' Bruce stated and then added, 'and what about you, are you married?'

'Yes,' replied Sarah in a subdued tone.

'And where does your husband work?' enquired Bruce.

'He's in business management, works for one of the firms in Duckingford.'

'No children yet?' asked Bruce.

'No,' said Sarah, still vouchsafing no more than she had to.

'So,' continued Bruce, detecting an embarrassing lull in the conversation, 'how do you spend your spare time? Any hobbies?'

'I busy myself,' replied Sarah and added, 'Clive,' referring to her husband, 'is an inveterate rock-climber. That's all he does at weekends. Sometimes I go along, sometimes I stay at home.'

There was another long pause and then Sarah appeared to change the conversation deliberately.

'So which school are you visiting this afternoon?'

'Three Lanes End in Barton Hope,' replied Bruce.

'You'll find it quite an experience,' commented Sarah. 'That's Amelia Trudgeon's school, an interesting but eccentric woman. Do you smoke?'

'Occasionally,' replied Bruce. 'My wife's gradually weaning me off the habit.'

'Well,' went on Sarah, 'if she likes you, Amelia may even offer you half a Woodbine.'

'You're joking,' said Bruce.

'Wait and see,' Sarah replied and she began to open the

car door, as if hinting it was time to get out.

'Yes, I must get a quick sandwich downtown and then hurry off to Barton Hope,' said Bruce.

'I may see you downtown,' Sarah replied. 'But first, I've got some work in the office. Anyway, have a nice afternoon.'

Bruce felt in high spirits as he made his way to a nearby café. He was getting to know people and places in Monaston. It was a beautiful September day. Life was good, he felt. After a quick snack he collected his test material and other paraphernalia that educational psychologists carry around with them, and set off for the wilds of Barton Hope.

Although Three Lanes End Primary School was in the far north of the village, with the help of the map supplied by Harry Wilcox and some directions willingly given by a local postman, Bruce soon arrived at the gate of a very small school adjoining the local church. The school was run by two teachers and had no more than twenty pupils varying from five to eight years, all of whom were sitting cross-legged in the hall, listening to a story that was being read to them by Miss Trudgeon. Spotting Bruce tiptoeing through the hall, she stopped reading and called, 'Can I help you?'

Bruce fumbled in his case and pulled out the referral details of the child he wanted to see.

'I've come to see William Gilley,' he said.

'Ah, yes, you're the psychologist,' Amelia replied. 'Billy Gilley, where are you?' She located a rather apprehensive little boy with red hair and a face covered in freckles at the back of the group and instructed, 'Take this man to my office!' Turning to Bruce she added, 'Make yourself at home in there. If you need anything, Mrs Irons is in the kitchen. By the way, Billy's mother is coming in to see you at about half past two.'

Bruce was dutifully escorted to another room equipped

with desk, chairs and telephone. The clink of china could be heard from what appeared to be an adjoining kitchen. Quickly Bruce looked round the door of the kitchen and explained to the lady working there that he was the local authority educational psychologist who had come to carry out an assessment.

'Would you like a cup of coffee?' asked Mrs Irons.

'That would be nice,' replied Bruce, 'but could I have it after I've seen the little boy?'

'Very well,' answered Mrs Irons and Bruce closed the door to reduce the amount of noise.

By this time Billy Gilley was sitting at the desk waiting with keen anticipation. Bruce quickly arranged his various test materials and decided to commence the assessment with a spelling and writing test. Billy was eight years old and had been referred to the Psychological Service on account of difficulties he was experiencing with handwriting. His teachers described him as an apparently bright child who could not get things down on paper.

Bruce offered Billy a pencil and instructed him to write his name at the top of a piece of lined paper which was placed in front of him. Bruce noted immediately that Billy manipulated the pencil with his left hand, and like many left-handed people who had not received appropriate instruction in handwriting, he hooked his arm around the top of the page when writing. In contrast to a right-handed person who pulls his pencil across the page from left to right and can thereby see his work as it is completed, the left-handed writer is forced to push his writing implement across the page in the same direction and as he does so, he thereby obscures his work as he completes it. To overcome this, many left-handed people hook their writing arm around the top of the page with the shaft of the pencil pointing away from them. Once a child adopts this habit and is allowed to do so, it can be very difficult to correct.

The habit can also result in muscle fatigue, stiffness of the joints and writer's cramp.

During his training as an educational psychologist, Bruce had made a special study of left-handed people and he always carried with him the relevant guides and equipment to help such individuals. He was secretly delighted whenever he came across a 'left-hander' and so had the opportunity of demonstrating his specialist knowledge of the subject.

As Billy completed the spelling test, Bruce observed that the child was inclined to letter reversals. This is common with very young children but normally should not persist over the age of seven. Billy wrote 'dit' instead of 'bit' and 'bown' instead of 'down'. Bruce also noted a tendency to mis-order and transpose letters. The child had written 'brid' for 'bird', and 'gril' for 'girl'. These were typical examples of a child who was suffering from a degree of specific learning difficulty in written language. The condition is sometimes referred to as 'dyslexia' and although Bruce was always happy to describe it thus, he was aware that many people in educational circles were not only sceptical, but at times openly hostile to accepting the existence of the problem. Dyslexia at that time had long been accepted in America but in Britain it was still customary to describe it as a middle-class syndrome.

As the assessment session continued, Bruce administered further diagnostic tests. Billy's intelligence came out in the above-average range, and in non-verbal or spatial and constructional tasks he showed particularly high abilities. His scores in reading and spelling, however, suggested that he was operating over two years behind his age level in these areas. The diagnostic tests indicated that Billy had problems with short-term memory and he also appeared to be a child of mixed laterality. Whilst he wrote with his left hand, he held a kaleidoscope up to his right eye. He kicked a football with his right leg and preferred to listen to a working stopwatch with his left ear. Mixed or cross laterality is a common feature in the profiles of children with learning problems in literacy skills. The relationship is neither clear nor consistent but the child may experience difficulties with orientation and sequencing and these can contribute to a delay in the acquisition of skills such as reading, spelling and writing.

As Bruce brought the testing session to an end, there was a knock on the door.

'Come in,' Bruce shouted and a lady opened the door and entered. She was modestly dressed in a blue jumper and skirt to match, and carried a handbag.

'I'm Billy's mother,' she announced.

'Ah, yes,' replied Bruce. 'I've just finished doing the tests. Billy can go back to his class now, and we can have a chat.'

Billy returned to his class and shortly afterwards the bell rang to signal the afternoon break. Within a couple of minutes Miss Trudgeon had joined Bruce and Mrs Gilley, and all three were able to discuss Bruce's test results over a cup of coffee.

Like many psychologists, Bruce always believed in highlighting the good news about a child first.

'I gave Billy an intelligence test,' he said, 'and as far as I am concerned, he comes in the above-average range. In other words, he has good intelligence.'

'He's quite bright,' interjected Mrs Gilley.

Miss Trudgeon said nothing.

'Yes, there is certainly nothing wrong with his intelligence,' continued Bruce. 'Billy's arithmetic is also not bad. He is what we call "age appropriate", that is, he is working near his age level in number work.

'Billy's problems, as I am sure you are both aware, are to do with reading, writing and spelling. He has special difficulties in these areas,' Bruce went on, 'and it's my feeling that he has what is called a specific problem with literacy skills. It's sometimes called "dyslexia" and up to twelve per cent of people have a degree of it. One thing with dyslexia is that we know it runs in families. Tell me, Mrs Gilley, is there anyone else in the family who has difficulty with spelling?'

'My husband does,' replied Mrs Gilley immediately. 'If there's any writing to be done, I have to do it. If he tries to write a letter it takes him all day. It's like wading through treacle.'

'Where does he work?' asked Bruce.

'Down the mine like most men around here. He's a mining engineer.'

'Ah,' said Bruce. 'Doesn't surprise me, Mrs Gilley. Dyslexia does not always mean there is something wrong with your brain. It's not a brain defect but rather a brain difference. Some of the most famous engineers, architects, scientists and artists had difficulty with spelling, for example Michael Faraday, Albert Einstein and lots of famous people today,' and with that Bruce produced a large walnut from his case. He kept it there to be used as a visual aid when the occasion demanded it.

'You see this?' he said. 'It's a walnut and it's shaped very much like our brain, that is, it has two halves.'

By this time, both Mrs Gilley and Amelia Trudgeon were listening intently.

Bruce continued, 'The one on the right we call the right hemisphere and the one on the left we call the left hemisphere. The right side deals with spatial, constructional and mechanical abilities, such as those used by engineers, architects and artists, and the left side is concerned more with the nitty-gritty of language and logic. When we learn to read, write and spell, we use the left side of the brain. The right side governs the left side of the body and vice versa. So if you have an accident and the left side of your brain is damaged, you may lose the power of speech and you may become paralysed in the right arm and right leg. The brain, of course, is a lot more complicated than that but that's a simple way of putting it and this appears true for most people. Now, what I noticed about Billy was that he had above-average intelligence and he shows particularly high abilities in working out what we call spatial tasks, such as puzzles.'

'He's always been good at Lego,' said Mrs Gilley.

'I'm not surprised,' replied Bruce. 'What Billy requires is special help with his reading, spelling and writing and that doesn't mean more of the same teaching he is already getting. It means a special kind of help, a special kind of teaching,' emphasised Bruce.

'Dyslexics learn best by a method which is very carefully graded and reading, spelling and writing are all taught at the same time, or simultaneously, so that the one reinforces the other. The approach has a highfalutin psychological name. It's called a "structured phonic approach based upon multi-sensory methods". Don't be put off by the name. It's really common sense when you look at it.

'Some children pick up reading and spelling easily. They see a word and they can remember it. But others, although they have good intelligence, have great difficulty in remembering words, and it's our job to make it easier for them, to teach them special ways of working out what the words say.' Bruce produced a small set of books and flash cards from his case. Waving the pack in front of Mrs Gilley and Miss Trudgeon, he said, 'I shall now show you how it is done.'

Bruce opened the first book and pointed to the first page. 'You teach the child that the letter a is for ant.' Bruce emphasised the short vowel sound and not the long one. 'How does he remember that? Don't tell me,' Bruce went on. 'You use your memory, of course. What do you mean by memory?' he continued. 'The roads to the memory are through the ears,' and Bruce pointed to his ears, 'and the eyes or vision,' and Bruce pointed to his eyes. 'So you hear the letter sound and the word and you see the picture of the ant and the word. But,' and here Bruce pointed to the bottom of the page, 'above all, you write it, and we call this the motor memory. What goes into the motor memory is often difficult to unlearn and that is precisely why our poor little Billy is hooking his arm and hand across the top of the page when he writes. He taught himself to do that and it has become a bit of a habit. It has gone into the motor memory. So, both good things and bad things can go into the motor memory.'

'So you teach that a is for ant,' Bruce repeated again and pointed at the picture and word on the first page of the book. 'What you don't teach the child who is beginning to read is that a is for arm. The word arm is taught in Workbook 6,' continued Bruce whilst picking up the appropriate book, 'when you teach the family of car words. Oh, here they are, car words,' he said, opening the book at the appropriate page. 'What you also do not teach is what we were taught, namely that a is for apple. The word apple is quite confusing for the young children with those sticks or lines going up and down. Apple is taught in Workbook 9,' and Bruce opened Workbook 9 from his teaching pack and disclosed a page entitled 'The Apple Family'. Bruce turned the page over and said, 'We must not forget the writing. Here the child can transfer the words from the box below to the appropriate picture.'

'There's a lot more to talk about in this pack but basically what you are doing is using a step-by-step approach to the teaching of reading, writing and spelling. Remember you are using your auditory memory,' he said, pointing to his ears, 'your visual memory,' he pointed to his eyes, 'and above all, your motor memory, when you write words,' he repeated, picking up a pencil.

'It's my belief that all children should be taught this way but particularly those like Billy who have special learning difficulties which are nothing to do with his intelligence.'

'So why can't my Billy be taught this way?' asked Mrs Gilley.

'No reason at all,' replied Bruce, 'and I am sure that his teachers will be more than happy to work with you on this kind of programme.'

'Certainly,' agreed Miss Trudgeon, and at that point she took out a small packet of cigarettes from her apron pocket and asked Bruce and Mrs Gilley whether they would like half a Woodbine each. Bruce, concealing his amusement, politely declined. However, Mrs Gilley happily shared the small cigarette with Amelia.

'But there's another point which we should not forget,' Bruce went on. 'Billy has been failing for a long time and because of this, he has now developed negative attitudes towards his schoolwork and he has low self-esteem. Put it this way, if you and I can't do something very well, what do we do? We avoid it, don't we?'

'True,' said Mrs Gilley.

'Well,' Bruce continued, 'that's why it is so important now to build up Billy's self-esteem. How can we do that? Well here are some suggestions.' Bruce handed a little paperback entitled 'Self-esteem' over to Mrs Gilley. 'There are some good tips in this little book. I have a number of copies here. I am going to leave one for you and one for the teachers. You may find it helpful. I know that I have in the past.'

At this point Bruce began to draw the interview to a close.

'We will try to get as much help for Billy as possible and above all, the right kind of help. Are there any questions you would like to ask me?'

Although Mrs Gilley felt a little bewildered about all the new things she had learnt about her son, she managed to retain her self-composure, reflect a little and then ask Bruce, 'When will you be seeing Billy again?'

'Let's give it six months,' replied Bruce, 'and I will come back and check on Billy's reading and spelling ability to see if he is making satisfactory progress. Are you happy with that?'

'Yes,' replied Mrs Gilley, and with that, Bruce stood up and began to collect his materials together in preparation to depart. He shook hands with Mrs Gilley, bade farewell to both her and Miss Trudgeon, left the school and made towards the car park.

Although it was late in the afternoon, Bruce decided to return to the education office to check on his in-tray for any correspondence which might have come in during the afternoon. When he arrived at the office it was gone 5 p.m. and most of the staff had left. A cleaner was busy tidying up in the typing pool. Bruce went to his desk and picked up a small pile of letters and other documents in his in-tray. Three notes caught his attention. One was from Dr Harry Wilcox, another from Sarah Craig, the education welfare officer, and a third was from a certain Roger Judson who had helpfully put his occupation of police liaison officer beneath his signature. Harry had left his telephone number with a request for Bruce to ring him that evening. 'Nothing urgent,' he had written, 'just an idea which might interest you.'

Sarah Craig wished to discuss the case of two teenagers who were refusing to attend school, and Roger Judson wanted a chat about an incident Bruce had witnessed when he visited the gypsy encampment at Ruff Hollow. It could only be to do with the incident of the motorcyclists who had provoked Jumbo Lee, thought Bruce. But how did the police know so quickly? Perhaps Harry had informed Sergeant Judson about the incident. He recalled having mentioned it to Harry.

Bruce decided to follow up the enquiries from Sarah Craig and Roger Judson the next day, but he could respond to Harry's note immediately by ringing him on the number he had written on the note and which was presumably the telephone number of Harry's home.

Bruce took some time to get through to Harry. The line was engaged when he rang. Unknown to Bruce, Harry had been on the phone for over an hour discussing plans for the forthcoming hunt that Sunday. As a Master of the Hunt, it was Harry's job to see that it went as smoothly as possible. Through one of his many contacts on the Monaston grapevine, he had learnt that an all-out attempt had been planned to sabotage the hunt that weekend. An important line of defence, therefore, was to get as much support as possible in the hope that numbers could help neutralise the saboteurs' objectives.

Bruce was about to give up trying to contact Harry when, in a last attempt, he got through and heard his colleague's familiar voice on the line.

'You've had problems getting through? I'm not surprised,' said Harry. 'The phone's been very active tonight. Anyway, thanks for ringing. It's nothing urgent. You mentioned that your wife was coming over to Monaston this weekend to do some house-hunting with you.'

'Yes, it's all arranged,' said Bruce. 'Nanny, that's my mother-in-law, has agreed to look after the children.'

'Well,' continued Harry, 'after you have done your hunting for houses, why don't you come across to Hackford and see a real hunt? We start around 10 a.m. on Sunday and should finish in time for a drink and a snack at the Royal Oak, which incidentally is near the stables where we start out. Would you be interested?'

'We're both townees,' said Bruce. 'I am certainly interested in seeing another side of the area and my wife is always game – excuse the pun – to do something different. I've been wondering what kind of a surprise I could think up for her this weekend and you have now given me the answer.'

'Good,' exclaimed Harry. 'After we have been to the Royal Oak, you can both come back to my cottage, have a look at my masterpieces and have a cup of tea. So that's settled.'

'Many thanks,' said Bruce.

He was about to hang up, when Harry shouted, 'Wait, try to get some binoculars for Sunday. They are essential countryside accessories. And one more thing – we will be glad of your support. Rumour has it that the sabs will be trying to interfere with the hunt this weekend. See you soon.'

As Bruce put down the phone, he wondered whether the invitation to the action had been partly motivated by Harry's wish to increase the number of independent observers as defence against the saboteurs whom Bruce had already heard about.

It was getting late and Bruce was ready for his evening meal.

He left the building and made towards the shopping precinct, where he found a small restaurant.

Once he had eaten, Bruce returned to his hotel, wrote up his day's reports and before settling down to read a newspaper and watch television, he rang his wife. Marie did not appear in the happiest of moods. The children had been squabbling and the weather had prevented her taking them out. However, she mentioned one pleasing event. A young couple had expressed great interest in buying their house and they claimed that they already had a firm offer for their present house.

Marie also expressed interest in seeing the forthcoming hunt. She was looking forward to Saturday when she would be visiting Monaston for the first time.

Chapter Four
The Kiss of Life

The next day Bruce decided to get into his office early in order to deal with any incoming correspondence and contact Sarah Craig and Roger Judson before going out to see his first case. However, he had hardly settled down at his desk when Sarah arrived, closely followed by Roger.

With a flashing smile, Sarah said, 'Let me introduce you to Police Sergeant Roger Judson. Roger, this is Bruce Whitford.'

'A policeman without a uniform,' commented Bruce.

'Yes,' replied Roger. 'It's all part of public relations. We must not intimidate young offenders or their parents. I also prefer not to wear it.'

'Well, can you guess why we have come?' asked Sarah.

'Not a clue,' replied Bruce in wonderment.

'Well, we think that you have been involved in a robbery,' she continued.

Both Sarah and Roger were obviously enjoying the situation and affected a serious attitude.

'Go on,' said Bruce, at which point Roger interrupted.

'We'll get to the point,' he said. 'According to Jumbo Lee, you visited his site a couple of days ago.'

'Oh, the gypsy encampment? Yes,' replied Bruce.

'And you witnessed a fracas with a motorbike.'

'That's right,' replied Bruce, 'and if I remember correctly one of the yobbos who was trying to provoke Jumbo ended up escaping on the pillion of another bike at the cost of leaving his own behind. Jumbo wheeled it over to his caravan as I was driving away.'

'Good,' said Roger. 'That's exactly what I wanted to hear and what a good job you were around at the time! You see, the motorbike was in fact stolen property and I think I know who stole it. However, some of my colleagues are not over-enamoured with gypsies – they still see them as vagrants or nomads who sell pegs or steal babies. They are trying to pin the robbery on Jumbo Lee, but with your help I can prove them wrong. So, many thanks, Bruce.'

'Pleased to be of assistance,' replied Bruce.

At this point Sarah Craig joined in the conversation.

'The situation,' she said, 'is even more intriguing in fact. You see, I have a couple of teenage boys on my books for school refusal or truancy, call it what you like, and one of them, Johnny Hopper, Grasshopper to his friends, is known to be a motorbike thief. He wasn't at school on the day you saw the gang at Ruff Hollow and we have reason to believe that he could have been among the gang or even the one who left the bike and boot with Jumbo. We need to have a full psychological assessment on him as a preliminary to decide what we can do next. Would you be willing to see him in the near future?'

'As always, I'm at your service,' Bruce replied, smiling and opening his diary at the same time. 'What about next Wednesday afternoon, at about two?'

'I know this is cheeky,' interrupted Roger, 'but we need to follow up this lead concerning the motorbike as soon as possible. If you could see Johnny this Monday, it would be marvellous; we have a case conference on him next Thursday.'

'I'm fully booked on Monday,' replied Bruce, 'but if you like, I could fit him in tomorrow about three o'clock.'

'Wonderful,' exclaimed Roger. 'I will arrange for him to

be here on the dot of three.'

Bruce entered the name in his diary and added, 'And in the meantime you will let me have all his history and available notes?'

'Of course,' replied Roger. 'And if he is the same individual who left the motorbike at Ruff Hollow, would you be prepared to make a statement to that effect?'

'Why not?' replied Bruce.

'Thanks again,' said Roger. 'I must go now, so see you soon,' and he departed.

Bruce smiled at Sarah, who remained seated.

'I have another case which demands your help,' she said sheepishly, 'and in some ways this is an even stickier one.'

Bruce's eyes widened.

'It concerns a thirteen-year-old girl called Lydia Parfitt. She is the only child in a one-parent family. The history goes like this: the mother has never been married but some years ago she had a depressive period and went to see a psychiatrist. To cut a long story short, the psychiatrist told her to go away and have an emotional experience, and she did, and Lydia was the result.'

Bruce grinned. 'I like it,' he said.

'As a child,' Sarah continued, 'Lydia was completely indulged. She has a doting mother and a doting grandmother. She has had her own way throughout her life. Her mother has no control over her whatsoever and now, during the past few months, she has decided that she doesn't want to go to school. So she has become a school refusal case, not a classic one with anxiety and separation problems or a cry for help but, as I see it, a persistent and obstinate little brat. The cry for help in fact comes from her mother and ourselves. Lydia appears as tough as nails. The question is, how can we get her back to school?'

Bruce pondered. 'Perhaps our first task is to get her out of the home,' he suggested.

'Yes,' nodded Sarah. 'But how?'

'Well, here's a suggestion,' Bruce continued. 'We know that in a lot of cases school phobia is due not so much to the fact that the child dislikes the school or has a phobia about it, but that he or she has a problem in leaving home and separating from Mum or breaking the umbilical cord. Well, I know you said this is not a usual case of separation anxieties. So we could then be a little tough. Looking back at my work in the big city, I can remember a similar case in which a certain young teenage boy decided he didn't want to go to school. There were no obvious anxieties and I went along and tested him for intelligence and scholastic attainments. The testing, of course, was a bit of a charade. Afterwards, I informed the young man in question that he didn't have average intelligence, in many areas he was above average, in fact he was very clever, and that presented me with a problem because I now had to go back to the authorities and tell them that we couldn't make any excuses for him on account of low intelligence. In fact he had very good intelligence and as he knew he had to go to school by law and that by not going he was breaking the law, there was no alternative but to recommend that he was placed in a boarding school.

'He could, of course, come home sometimes at holiday times, I told him, but the holidays wouldn't be as long as his normal ones. Then I added with a suitable look of anxiety on my face, "I hope you are not going to blame me for this. I'm only doing my job." By this time the young man, I forget his name, was thoroughly confused. Whereupon I took some forms from my case and began to fill them out, indicating that these were the forms which would ultimately result in his placement somewhere else in the country. Having completed a few sections, I looked up and commented, "You are absolutely sure that you don't want to go back to school?" The next day the boy was back at school and we had no problems thereafter. On that occasion that approach worked and was appropriate. Of course it's not an approach I adopt for the majority of school refusals but it is worth considering. Do you think it would mean anything to Lydia?'

'We could try,' replied Sarah, 'since the alternative could be a care order from Social Services.'

'I'm quite flexible in the next hour or so. Shall we go and visit the home of this young lady right now?' Bruce suggested.

'Now?' replied Sarah, affecting an air of surprise.

'No time like the present,' replied Bruce and he gathered some letters and other documents in his case and they both departed to the car park at the back of the Town Hall.

'I know the way, so shall we go in my car?' volunteered Sarah.

'Good idea,' said Bruce and they both set off in Sarah's Ford Cortina across Monaston and out towards Dampstone where Lydia and her mother lived.

As they neared their destination, Bruce observed that the Dampstone area was not unlike Sockton. The names of the roads, Cedar Grove, Sycamore Avenue, Green Lane belied the dilapidated and, in some places, condemned buildings of the district. Sarah parked her car at the end of a cul-de-sac which rejoiced in the name of Pineapple Close.

'Just up here,' she indicated, and they walked towards the third of a group of terraced houses which were owned, like many others in the area, by the National Coal Board. They had been originally intended for the families of miners in the local mine.

Sarah rattled the letterbox on the front door, and eventually Lydia's mother appeared and invited them both in. Like most of the dwellings in the area, there was no reception hall or lobby. The outside door opened immediately into a rectangular-shaped room that was adequately and not untastefully furnished.

Miss Parfitt was known to be an intelligent lady who, whilst quietly spoken, could be firm and definite in her views. Rumour had it that she was the wayward daughter of a businessman from a nearby town, and that she had enjoyed a private education. Her cultured manner not only appeared a little incongruous with her surroundings but at times could be a little off-putting to professionals who were accustomed to the less sophisticated residents of that area of Monaston.

'So where's the little lady?' Sarah asked, sitting herself down on one of the two stout Edwardian chairs next to a table.

'Oh,' replied Miss Parfitt, 'my little progeny is in a state of repose at the moment. She has a headache. The late film last night was a rather noisy one.' She gesticulated towards the television.

'So Lydia is not too tired to stay up late at night to watch an adult film,' Bruce interjected, 'but she can't go to school in the morning.'

Miss Parfitt looked at Bruce questioningly. A new broom sweeps clean, she thought, but this could be an awkward one. She decided to divert the conversation a little.

'Dr Wilcox has been trying for years to secure Lydia's permanent attendance,' she went on. 'He would succeed for a time and then there would be another relapse.'

'I know the whole history,' replied Bruce, 'and quite frankly, I don't think I shall succeed either, so I will come to the point. You, like us all, want Lydia to have a regular education, don't you?'

'Of course,' answered Miss Parfitt, 'I would do anything to succeed there.'

Bruce paused and then resumed, 'We have discussed the whole case in great detail and there is only one approach left. As you know, I am new here but I am also experienced enough to know that where others have failed I will probably also fail, so what I am going to do is the following.

'First we need to get Lydia out of the house. It is not good for a child to be at home all the time. I shall try to arrange for her to attend a group at the Mutley Clinic as from tomorrow. I shall be there to greet her at a quarter to nine sharp. Now, to be frank, I do not believe Lydia will turn up tomorrow. So I have to do my job and part of it is to help your child to have a regular education to prepare her for when she grows up. If she refuses to come tomorrow, my next step is to complete forms to recommend that Lydia be placed in a boarding school for children with adjustment difficulties.'

'She won't like that,' replied Miss Parfitt.

'But they are very nice schools,' continued Bruce.

'Would you like to talk to her about this?' Miss Parfitt asked.

'Certainly,' replied Bruce. 'Tell her to come down here and we will discuss the situation in detail.'

Miss Parfitt rose and disappeared upstairs. Bruce gave Sarah a knowing wink, as if to say 'so far so good'. Within seconds, however, a rumpus occurred upstairs. Lydia could be heard screeching, 'Get out. I don't want to see him.'

Miss Parfitt appeared at the living room door. 'She won't get up,' she said dolefully. 'Do you think you could persuade her?'

Bruce and Sarah followed Miss Parfitt up the stairs to the first of two bedrooms. It was a small, square room and Lydia's bed occupied most of the area. The girl's head could be seen just above the blankets. She glared at the three of them as Bruce began.

'Lydia, I'm not asking you to get up,' he began, 'I'm just going to tell you what I have just told your mother. If you stay at home, you and your mother are both breaking the

The girl's head could be seen just above the blankets.

law. Now, I am not asking you to go to school tomorrow but I have arranged for you to go to a group at the Mutley Clinic. If you attend there regularly, the local authority will accept that this is the same as attending school and you and your mother will not be in trouble. However, if you do not turn up at Mutley tomorrow, I shall be forced to send these forms in, which means you will have to go to a boarding school. Mind you, don't get me wrong, you may well enjoy yourself at boarding school. There will be other children there like you who find it hard to go to school. But, of course, you won't get the long holidays which normal schools have.'

'How far away would a boarding school be?' enquired Lydia's mother.

'Truthfully, I don't know,' replied Bruce. 'It could be twenty miles or two hundred miles away. It depends where a suitable vacancy can be found. I visit one school in Suffolk which is nearly three hundred miles away. Now, I must fill out this form,' continued Bruce and he produced some documents from his case. His purpose was to make a meal of the procedure within earshot of the child in order to drive home the fact that he meant business.

'Firstly, let's get Lydia's full name correct. She is called Lydia,' and he wrote her first Christian name on the form. 'Are there any other Christian names?' asked Bruce.

'Yes,' replied Miss Parfitt. 'She is called Lydia Esmeralda Mason Parfitt; Mason is a family name.'

'Right. Now, the correct address?' asked Bruce.

'Number seven, Pineapple Close, Dampstone, Monaston,' replied Miss Parfitt.

'Good,' said Bruce, 'and finally Lydia's date of birth.'

'The 12th October, 1960,' she replied.

'Fine,' said Bruce, 'I can complete all the rest. Now before I go, let me make the situation quite clear,' Bruce's voice resounded through the house to the extent that Lydia could be under no misapprehension. 'If Lydia attends the group at the Mutley Clinic tomorrow, I shall not send this form in. However, if she stays away from the group at any time without a doctor's note, then the form goes in, and arrangements will be made for her to go to boarding school.'

'But,' replied Miss Parfitt, 'suppose Lydia refuses to go to the boarding school.'

'Oh, that's not my responsibility,' replied Bruce. 'She then becomes the concern of Social Services who will take her from her home and place her in the care of the local authority.' With that, he closed his document case and bade farewell to Lydia and her mother.

'I'm gasping for a coffee,' said Bruce as he climbed into the passenger side of Sarah's car.

'Do you want one back at the office or downtown?' she asked.

'Anywhere,' said Bruce.

'There's a little café next to the post office on Hill Top. It's not far from the Town Hall, so we could go there,' suggested Sarah.

It wasn't long before Sarah had parked her car at a safe distance from the bus stop on the crown of Hill Top, which was on the south side of Monaston. From it much of the borough could be observed.

On entering the café, Bruce ordered two coffees.

'This is my treat, you've been doing the driving,' he said. They sat opposite one another at one of the two little square tables in the window of the café. After a couple of minutes of staring at each other, the conversation began to flow more smoothly. Sarah appeared more forthcoming than the previous day. From Bruce's initial question concerning which part of the country she came from, Bruce soon learnt that Sarah was an only child who had been brought up in a small Yorkshire town. She had been married for three years and had met her husband in Leeds, where she was studying sociology and he was studying business management. They had come to Monaston when he had been offered a post in one of the big Midland car factories nearby. Although based in the Midlands, Clive, her husband, seemed to spend a great deal of his time travelling around the country, and at weekends he often went rock-climbing, she told him. Sarah complained that she saw little of him but was lucky to have a number of friends and a fair social life.

In turn, Sarah learnt that Bruce was married with three children. He too had met his wife when at university, and after some years spent teaching, he had qualified as an educational psychologist and had worked in the London area for a few years before accepting his present post.

Sarah and Bruce were so engrossed in conversation that neither of them noticed Delia Berry draw up on Hill Top, alight from her car and post a letter. She spotted them in the window. 'Food for thought,' she muttered to herself as she quickly returned to her car.

'Well, we now know something about each other,' Bruce remarked as the coffee session came to a close.

'Yes,' replied Sarah and added, 'and we have something in common, namely the case of Lydia Parfitt. If you can help me solve that one, it will certainly take a weight off my mind.'

Sarah dropped Bruce off at the front entrance of the Town Hall and they both went their separate ways, he to his office and she to a local school. On entering the office, Bruce noticed that Harry Wilcox was engaged in conversation at the door of his room with a middle-aged and apparently very articulate lady.

Seeing Bruce, Harry beckoned to him. 'Have you met Delia?' he said.

'No, I haven't had the pleasure as yet,' replied Bruce,

adding, 'but your reputation has preceded you.'

'Yes,' added Harry, 'Delia is the eyes, nose and ears of the Service. She's a psychiatric social worker, investigator and spy *extraordinaire* all rolled into one.'

'That's true,' interjected Delia and, looking at Bruce, she asked, 'Did you enjoy your coffee with Sarah at Hill Top?'

Bruce had hardly recovered from the shock of having been spied upon when Harry's secretary interrupted the conversation.

'I'm sorry to disturb you, Dr Wilcox, but Sir Giles Pemberton is on the phone.'

Harry rushed to his office. 'Hullo Giles, and a good morning to you,' he said.

'So far it has been a terrible morning, Harry,' Sir Giles replied, 'and to cap it all, I understand that the Sabs intend to ruin our hunt this weekend. What do you think? We've tricked them before. Can we do it again?'

Harry pondered. 'I have heard rumours to that effect,' he said, 'and I've already been taking some precautionary measures. The trouble is that there is not a great deal that one can do if they try to get at the hounds. I'll explore further possibilities and get back to you.'

As Harry put down the phone, his eyes alighted on his favourite print, *Las Meniñas* by Velázquez. This weekend may well be a colourful one, he thought.

Meanwhile, Bruce had gone to his own office and phoned Doris Dicker to prepare her for the possible attendance of Lydia Parfitt in her adjustment unit the next day. He knew that there was a space in her group for urgent cases and with suitable flattery he managed to enlist Doris's support in trying to secure Lydia's attendance. 'If anyone can straighten this child out it's you,' said Bruce.

'Don't worry if she doesn't attend – I'll drag her here,' replied Doris, who relished a challenge.

Monaston was enjoying an Indian summer that year and

when Bruce met his wife, Marie, at the borough's only railway station around midday on Saturday, the weather was as good as one could wish for an introduction to one's future home town. After a quick embrace, Bruce took Marie's travel bag and announced, 'It's market day in Monaston today, so we'll go through that way, leave your bag at the hotel and then get a quick snack, and then off we go house-hunting. How's that?'

'Sounds good to me,' replied Marie.

Bruce had not brought the car with him since the High Street was closed to traffic on market day, and he thought the circuitous route back to his hotel, which avoided the centre of town, would have taken only a little less time than the direct walk through the market. As it happened, Marie, who had had little experience of a small-town market found many of the stalls fascinating. Whilst she was engrossed in a toy stall, Bruce saw a young scallywag carefully trying to pocket a toy car. Bruce drew the attention of the stall owner to what was happening and she immediately yelled and made a grab for the boy who quickly slipped away into the crowd.

'I recognise him,' she exclaimed. 'One of the Kelly family! They're all thieves. Little varmints!'

Meanwhile, a few yards away, a mother was dragging a screaming four-year-old away from the toy display and smacking him harshly at the same time. A bystander remarked sharply to the mother, 'If you did that to an adult, Madam, you would find yourself in court for assault.'

Bruce at once recognised the voice; it was none other than Harry Wilcox. Their eyes met.

'What a coincidence,' said Bruce. 'May I introduce you to my wife, Marie? What brings you here?'

'I never miss market day,' replied Harry. 'Best bargains in Monaston. I normally load myself with sustenance for the week here. Good food and vegetables. I've also picked

She immediately yelled and made a grab for the boy who slipped away into the crowd.

up the odd bargain antique in this place. I won't keep you. You are no doubt going house-hunting. Watch your handbag and pockets. Look forward to seeing you both tomorrow,' and with that, he disappeared into the crowd.

If first impressions are important, then Marie's introduction to Monaston was a success. At the hotel she remarked how useful such a market could be for a young family.

'At least I shall know where to get fresh fruit and vegetables for the week,' she said, 'and they're quite cheap compared with home.'

Bruce had arranged two visits to houses that afternoon. The first was not a great success and Bruce sensed why – it only had three bedrooms. One of the attractions of moving house for Marie was the possibility of living in a four-bedroom house. As the family was growing, they could make good use of an extra bedroom. They would also need this to accommodate visitors during holidays. Bruce also appreciated the possibility of an extra room as it could provide him with a study.

The second house they viewed was on the Hatley estate. It not only had four bedrooms but there was a loft extension which further enhanced its value. Since they arrived a little early Bruce and Marie sat outside the apparently empty, but not unattractive, detached property. Within minutes two cars approached from opposite directions and parked on either side of theirs. 'Obviously a two-car family,' remarked Bruce. 'Their name is Hawkins, according to my papers here from the estate agent.' They watched the couple enter the house separately and then they ventured forth and knocked on the door. It was opened by the lady who introduced herself and shook hands with Marie and Bruce. The man, who seemed to be busy in the kitchen, appeared later and introduced himself.

It was not long before Bruce and his wife sensed a

strained atmosphere between the couple, who hardly communicated with each other throughout. The garden at the back was spacious and relatively tidy given that it had obviously not been looked after for some weeks. Among other things it contained a shed, a swing and children's climber.

'Are those part of the fixtures?' asked Bruce.

'If you want them you're welcome,' replied Mrs Hawkins. 'My children spent many happy hours out there.'

There was a feeling of nostalgia mingled with sadness in her voice.

By this time both Marie and Bruce had sensed that the tension arose from the fact that the couple were breaking up their relationship and probably heading for divorce, hence the reason for the house being up for sale.

'What are the schools like around here?' enquired Marie. 'You see, we have three young children.'

'The standards are good,' replied Mrs Hawkins. 'Both my children attended the local infants and junior schools and did well. There is also a sixth form college not far away.'

Both Bruce and Marie were impressed with the house, and recognised its potential from the point of view of their young family. As prospective buyers, both had agreed not to show too much enthusiasm since this might affect negotiations.

'If we want to make an offer I assume that we write to the agents?' enquired Bruce.

'Yes, that's the procedure,' interjected Mr Hawkins, who until then had been largely reticent.

Bruce and Marie bade farewell to the owners and returned to their car where they were able to voice their thoughts.

'Don't tell me,' said Bruce, 'you deduced that they were splitting up.'

'What else?' replied Marie. 'Anyway, that's their business. What did you think of the house?'

'Tailor-made for our needs: a playroom downstairs, a nice garden and a nice study where I can work.' Bruce had his tongue in his cheek as he added the latter.

'That's all you're interested in – your study,' replied Marie with a smile.

'Do you want me to make a bid?' asked Bruce. 'We can afford the asking price but of course, I shall bid lower.'

'Not too low,' replied Marie, 'or we may miss it. Dad said that the secret is to get them interested.'

Bruce remained silent. He reflected that he was well able to make his own decisions without advice from inlaws, helpful as they were.

'At least we don't seem to have the problem of selling our own house,' said Marie. 'The young couple who are first-time buyers are adamant that they want it.'

'Don't count your chickens. Nothing is certain about house-buying,' said Bruce. 'Remember our experiences when we bought our present one. Anyway, I shall make a bid at the estate agents on Monday and tell them that we have a good chance of selling our present property easily.'

Sunday morning arrived. Although a little duller than the previous day, the weather was fine enough to watch the fox-hunt. Marie and Bruce arrived early at the stables of Pyper's Farm where the hunt was scheduled to begin. They were equipped with both field glasses and a camera. Cars and motorcycles were scattered up and down the road leading to the entrance to the stables, and among the onlookers Bruce distinguished two familiar faces – Roger Judson, the police liaison officer, and Doris Dicker, head of the unit for disturbed children at Mutley.

Whilst Bruce was introducing Marie to Roger Judson, Doris Dicker came up and thrust a leaflet entitled 'Protect Our Wildlife' into Bruce's hands. On this occasion Doris was wearing wellington boots and luminous socks.

'Are you working or watching?' Bruce questioned Roger.

'Both really,' replied Roger. 'Dr Wilcox asked me if I could be here to help quell any disturbances that may arise.'

'They look fairly harmless to me,' Bruce remarked, gazing at the scattered onlookers.'

'They always do,' replied Roger. 'But what do you think those youths are carrying in their long pockets and what about that eccentric-looking gentleman with the walking stick and topper? What has he got under his hat? Sabs come in all shapes and sizes.'

'I suppose they do,' replied Bruce, looking around for Doris Dicker, who by this time, along with a small group of sabs, appeared to be leaving the scene and crossing a nearby field.

Just then the noise in the stable yard seemed to gain momentum and the regular clip-clop of hooves on cobbles became louder with the odd yelp from the hounds. All eyes turned to the entrance of Pyper's Farm, as the hunt emerged, led by the huntmaster who was closely followed by Harry Wilcox and the other huntsmen in full regalia, with the hounds at their feet. A number of farmhands were in close contact with the hounds and the leader of the pack was on a leash, as were several other experienced hounds.

'This is where the fun begins,' said Roger, leaving quickly to take up a more strategic position farther down the road.

As the hounds approached, the eccentric-looking man took off his hat and reached for a packet on top of his head. Before his hand reached it, however, an arm from a brawny farmhand who had advanced behind him, reached out, grabbed the packet of raw meat and flung it far and high back into the farmyard.

'I'll have you arrested!' yelled the man in astonishment.

'Don't know what you mean, sir,' replied the farmhand as he moved farther down the road towards a small group of likely saboteurs.

By this time, yells of derision were rising from various spectators scattered down the lane; 'Wilcox Killfox' seemed to be a popular catcall.

Sir Giles Pemberton and his colleagues were well aware of the tactics of the sabs, who had been busy smearing and scattering pieces of raw meat on the ground and around the adjacent fields in their attempt to divert and confuse the pack. However, they also knew that such diversions had their limitations. The hunt could afford to lose a few hounds on the way as long as they retained control over the leaders of the pack, and this is what they seemed to be doing.

A dog fox had left his morning scent near a gate. The opportunity was there. The gate was quickly opened and most of the chase sped through across the fields towards Blackberry Water, a small lake often frequented by local anglers. It was this spot that Doris Dicker and a small group of sabs clad in wellingtons had been making for. The ground became softer and almost marshy in places as the hunt approached the borders of the lake.

Suddenly the hounds began to slow down and scatter. They had picked up the scent of the raw meat scattered over the field by the group of sabs. In an effort to slow his horse Harry Wilcox tugged on its reins, the horse came to an abrupt halt and Harry at once went hurtling through the air, somersaulting and landing prostrate in the mud. As he lay motionless for a few seconds, the crowd jeered. Doris Dicker's face was a mixture of concern and amazement. Their plan had worked but not in the way she had anticipated. Despite her faults and her many criticisms of Harry Wilcox, Doris had a soft heart under her rough exterior. Seeing one of her colleagues in dire trouble, she yelled,

'Emergency!' and rushed towards the mud-spattered body of Harry. On reaching him, she loosened his collar, took off his riding hat and proceeded to give Harry the kiss of life. As their faces met at the closest of quarters, Harry's eyes opened and seeing Dicker's visage closer than he had ever seen it, he appeared to fall into a dead faint.

By this time the news of the incident had been relayed to the onlookers near the farm. Marie had seen everything through her field glasses. She yelled to Roger Judson who, in a flash, was in his car and radioing for an ambulance.

When Monday morning arrived, the whole of the education office was agog with the news of the hunt. People were reading newspaper reports on the subject, and Harry's secretary was busy cancelling his appointments and rearranging his timetables. Bruce had arranged to visit Harry that lunchtime. Despite the front page headline of the *Monaston Spectator*, which read, 'Hunt Sabs cause near fatal accident', the overall news was good. Harry was comfortable in hospital and, as far as was known, had only sustained a fractured femur.

Bruce's first visit that day was to Sockton Infants School where he had arranged to assess the strange case of a little girl of six years who supposedly had refused all verbal communication with her teachers and other adults at the school since she had started there approximately a year ago. The teachers, including the headmistress, were sceptical that she was able to speak at all, although on occasion she was reported to have spoken to other children in the playground. Her communication problem had also been circumvented to some extent by a close friend who conveyed her wishes to others. The little girl was obviously intelligent, since she had few problems carrying out instructions and was able to do her schoolwork. Her worried and anxious mother had on one occasion produced a tape of the child conversing at home for the teachers to hear.

As in many schools, Bruce conducted his interview in the head teacher's office. He spread out a number of puzzles on the head teacher's desk in the hope of exciting the child's interest. The little girl, who was called Kerry Baker, was brought in by one of the classroom assistants. She was an attractive little girl with dark hair and brown eyes. She sat on the chair beside Bruce who, for the next fifteen minutes, tried every trick he could think of to encourage the child to participate in solving a series of little tasks but she adamantly refused to speak or contribute to the activities.

Cases of this nature were not common, but fortunately Bruce had learnt about them in his training and had come across the odd one before. He considered it pointless to prolong the interview and, having returned the child to her classroom, discussed the problem over coffee with the child's mother and Miss Hawton, the head teacher.

'It appears to be a case of elective mutism,' pronounced Bruce in a fairly authoritative manner, although he was well aware of the dangers of an over-hasty diagnosis involving a language problem. 'It's basically a condition which is associated with specific situations. The child is so overwhelmed by a situation that she refuses to use, or indeed cannot use language when in that situation. In Kerry's case the situation is school.'

Both Mrs Baker and Miss Hawton looked perplexed.

'So what happens now?' asked Mrs Baker.

'Well,' continued Bruce, 'I want you to bring her into my office tomorrow at about 3 p.m. and I will see if Kerry's reactions are different. In short I want to find out if she will converse with me in a totally different situation. If she does, we shall have established that it is a case of elective mutism and we shall then set up a programme to encourage Kerry to speak in her school situation. It won't, of course, be easy.

I cannot wave a magic wand, but we can only try. If that doesn't work then I shall approach the speech therapy department and will consider the possibility of help from the speech and language unit which is attached to the Westfield School. Meanwhile, the answer is to relax. Don't become over-anxious, since that will not help Kerry. Encourage her to participate as much as possible in school activities as well.

Both the head teacher and the child's mother seemed visibly relieved as they bade farewell to Bruce. At least they felt that something was at last being done.

Bruce's next destination was the local hospital. On arriving there, he was taken to a private room where Harry Wilcox was sitting up in bed checking his shares in the business section of a daily quality newspaper.

'Hello,' said Harry, catching sight of Bruce. He looked both pleased and surprised to see him.

'You're in luxury,' remarked Bruce, glancing at the television and other mod cons in the room.

'Just retrieving some of the benefits of a well-paid health insurance,' replied Harry.

'Well, what's the verdict?' asked Bruce.

'It appears that I have a fractured femur. I need to take it easy for a few weeks,' said Harry. 'It won't interfere too much with my work, apart from one little hitch, and I am hoping that you can help me here, Bruce.'

'Fire away,' replied Bruce.

'Well you see, next weekend, along with Jesse Fry, the education welfare officer, I have arranged to attend a conference on Asperger's Syndrome down south and now I can't go.'

'Oh!' exclaimed Bruce.

Harry continued, 'Can you take my place and go along with Jesse? Take copious notes, draw up a detailed report on the conference and collect as many handouts as possible along with any other literature.'

'It sounds interesting,' replied Bruce, 'and I certainly could do with brushing up my knowledge on Asperger's Syndrome, which is on the autistic continuum, I believe. Isn't Asperger's a high ability autistic, identified many years ago by a German of the same name?'

'You're with it,' answered Harry with a gleam in his eye, adding, 'Like the dyslexics, there are probably many of these children around who are being wrongly diagnosed as having behavioural or conduct disorders and as a consequence are also being wrongly treated. Some say that the comedian, Peter Sellers, shows signs of Asperger's Syndrome, and many adults who have odd hobbies, such as collecting train numbers, could be examples of the same condition.'

As Bruce drove back to the office he felt particularly pleased to have the opportunity to attend a conference on a subject which was one of the chinks in his armour of psychological knowledge. It would also be a good opportunity to make first-hand contact with a member of the Education Welfare Service whom he did not know very well. He had been introduced to Jesse Fry when he first arrived in Monaston. He recalled Jesse as being a friendly, corpulent and laid-back individual who moved down the corridor as if he were wearing carpet slippers. One of the education officers had also informed Bruce that Jesse's nickname among the local truants and school refusals was Bellybutton, possibly on account of his protruding middle-age spread.

As coincidences occur, Jesse Fry was in fact padding down the corridor when Bruce arrived in the Council House.

'I feel sorry for you, Jesse,' said Bruce as they approached one another.

Jesse looked perplexed.

'You've got to put up with me next weekend at the Asperger's Conference,' Bruce explained. 'I'm taking Harry Wilcox's place.'

'Marvellous,' replied Jesse with a twinkle in his eye. 'Maybe we can have a few jars together.'

'Dr Wilcox did all the arrangements for the conference, Jesse added. 'I haven't a clue what it's about. You live and learn – I hope I learn something!'

As they were talking, Sarah Craig brushed past them, apparently deep in thought and hardly acknowledging either Bruce or Jesse.

'Sarah's a bit confused at the moment,' whispered Jesse. 'Matrimonial problems, I believe. Her husband's off to America for six months. He's been seconded by his firm, I understand.' He added in a whisper, 'Some say it's a trial separation. They haven't been getting on for months. The rumour is that she wants children and he doesn't. Anyway, let's hope things work out.' With that, Jesse bade farewell and Bruce went into his office to go through his post and arrange some further appointments.

The next day Bruce arrived early at the Council House. He wanted to make some further phone calls and do some administration before the visit of Kerry Baker, the little girl whom he had diagnosed as having elective mutism. Her visit was scheduled for 3 p.m. The appointment soon arrived and Bruce welcomed Kerry and her mother into the outer office. Mrs Baker was given a chair and Bruce took Kerry into his office to attempt some tests. He did so with trepidation, half-expecting the interview to collapse as the previous one had. To Bruce's delight, however, Kerry became quite talkative, in fact almost garrulous at times. She spoke about her pet cat, Bubbles, who had nearly been run over the week before. It was her birthday soon and Bruce learnt that she was having a party and was going to invite a number of friends.

During the conversation Bruce heard the familiar voice of Sarah Craig in the office. It flashed through his mind that Sarah could act as a useful witness to Kerry's ability to converse freely in certain situations. He knew, like her mother, that some of the teachers at the school still doubted Kerry's ability to speak at all. Sockton Infants School was on Sarah's patch. Perhaps he could enlist her help both as a witness and in the treatment of the child. The post of education welfare officer now included other responsibilities than merely securing school attendance.

Bruce gave Kerry a puzzle to do and opened his door. Seeing Sarah going through some letters he briefly explained the situation to her and the girl's mother.

'You see,' he said, 'Kerry will not converse in a school situation, she refuses to speak a single word. Isn't that so, Mrs Baker?'

Kerry's mother nodded.

'And yet,' continued Bruce, 'today I can't stop her talking in my office.'

Mrs Baker looked delighted. It had worked after all!

'Now first I want you to witness her conversation with me,' said Bruce to Sarah, 'and, as Kerry attends one of your schools, would it be possible to enlist your help in helping her overcome the problem?'

'Always willing to oblige,' replied Sarah, following Bruce into his office where a three-way conversation ensued.

After the conversation Kerry was again left in Bruce's office with some challenging puzzles to complete while Bruce, Sarah and Mrs Baker discussed a plan whereby Sarah would meet Kerry and her mother outside the school on a number of consecutive mornings. The aim would be to keep Kerry talking as she walked through the school gates and into the cloakroom, and, if possible, down the corridor and into the classroom. It was accepted that

Kerry's school behaviour would not change radically overnight, so a process of gradual conditioning was to be followed and closely monitored. Sarah would keep Bruce informed of any progress that was made.

As Kerry and her mother were leaving the office, Jesse Fry looked in and asked Bruce how they proposed to travel to the conference that Friday afternoon.

'I'm quite happy to use my car,' said Bruce, 'unless you prefer to use yours.'

'No, that's fine. I'm quite happy to be a passenger,' replied Jesse.

It was settled that Bruce would meet Jesse in his office early on Friday afternoon and they would travel together in Bruce's car to the conference. They estimated that the journey would take about two hours.

Chapter Five

A Case of Asperger's Syndrome

Friday afternoon soon arrived. Jesse Fry and Bruce Whitford set off with a map, each taking a travelling bag with him. The weather was fine and their aim was to stop halfway for a snack. They were soon heading south on the motorway. Jesse had the map on his lap and was acting as navigator.

The journey went smoothly and after about twenty minutes they soon became engrossed in conversation. The subject changed from previous jobs which both had had, to their respective families. Bruce learnt that Jesse had four children. Two were at university, a girl studying medicine, a boy involved with computers. There was another child, a teenage girl, who was still at school. Finally, there was a boy named Tom, who had apparently been a problem throughout his school life.

Tom had always been something of a loner. As a young child, he had angelic features and adults often made a fuss of him. One teacher however had said that he was the most complex child she had ever taught. Tom's problems came to a head at the start of his teenage years. Like his siblings he had attended the local comprehensive school. On one occasion he had actually hit a teacher and Jesse felt that it was only his own position in the education office that had prevented the child from being suspended from school.

By the time Bruce and Jesse were enjoying a small snack

in a roadside café, Bruce had learnt that Jesse's son, Tom, had left school at sixteen, had tried a number of jobs and courses but each time the situation had broken down on account of relationship problems. At the age of eighteen, Tom disappeared and hadn't been seen since. That was nearly two years ago.

As he listened to the story, Bruce began to realise just how much stress and worry Jesse and his wife had been under over the years. Lying awake at night for hours wondering whether he was living like a tramp, taking drugs or involved in crime had become a way of life for the parents. They had already spent two Christmases without Tom.

'You haven't a clue where he is?' asked Bruce.

'I've followed up numerous leads but they have led nowhere,' replied Jesse.

'Have you tried the Salvation Army?' enquired Bruce.

'No,' replied Jesse, 'can they help?'

'Yes,' said Bruce. 'The Sally Army have ways and means of making contact with a missing person and they often succeed where others fail. For instance, I believe that they have a working relationship with the Department for Employment. Some people can be traced by means of registration or their National Insurance number. The Sally Army makes contact with missing people and delivers messages to them. If the person in question does not wish to be contacted then they will deliver your message but they will not divulge where the person is. They will respect his wishes. What I suggest is that when we get back to Monaston I will find the relevant address and we can work from there.' Jesse appeared visibly relieved and hopeful when he heard this information, and the rest of the journey was spent discussing a pursuit which they appeared to have in common, namely football.

Bruce and Jesse reached the conference hotel in time to

register and have an evening meal. This was followed by coffee and liqueurs in the bar, and then they both retired relatively early to their respective rooms.

Like many such functions, the conference on Asperger's Syndrome consisted of plenary sessions in the morning, followed by seminars and workshops in the afternoon. Bruce and Jesse attended separate workshops and arranged to swap notes during the evening. Although Jesse was not overfamiliar with some of the psychological terminology used in some of the lectures, his attention and interest became more intense as the conference progressed. One seminar was conducted by a speech therapist.

As the young lady enumerated the classic symptoms of a child with Asperger's Syndrome, Jesse gradually realised that she was describing his son, Tom. It was as if she actually knew him.

'Eye contact,' she said, 'is often a give-away.' These children have poor eye contact. Often it is fleeting, while on occasion they may stare hard into your eyes when trying to make a definite point.'

Tom's eye contact was never normal, thought Jesse.

'Many have monomania or obsessions with objects or ideas.'

Jesse thought of Tom's obsession as a child with cars and later, lions.

'Another symptom is making inappropriate remarks,' the speaker went on. 'These children appear to lack tact or common sense and can make embarrassing remarks in company.'

This again was so true of Tom. Jesse recalled how on one occasion they had been travelling on a bus and Tom had yelled out, 'My dad's name is Bellybutton.' He was eight years old at the time. On another occasion in a supermarket he went up to a rather corpulent lady and asked her how much she weighed.

'These children are often good looking,' she continued.

Tom was undoubtedly the best-looking person in the Fry family. As a young child he had been invited to model clothes for a local photographer.

'As they grow older these children sometimes become preoccupied with the macabre,' she said.

This clinched it. Jesse recalled how his wife had found numerous newspaper cuttings in Tom's bedroom of the Yorkshire Ripper and other murderers. He also seemed unhealthily preoccupied with the subject of the Holocaust. At the time it had given them a great deal of worry. By this time Jesse's eyes were becoming watery. At last he was beginning to understand his wayward son.

Tom suffered from a developmental disorder which was known as Asperger's Syndrome. Children with this condition perceive life entirely differently. It was not their fault, it was the way they were made. All those criticisms from the family, teachers and others in the past had been unfair. What Tom had needed during his childhood was understanding and treatment and, like many similar cases, he had missed out because his problem had not been properly diagnosed or understood.

It suddenly struck Jesse that this was why Dr Wilcox had insisted that he attended the conference. Harry was as crafty as the foxes he chased. He knew about Tom although he had never been involved in his case himself. Since Tom's disappearance, Jesse had on occasion opened his heart to Harry, who had used his professional insight on the basis of mere descriptions of his child's behaviour. Now it all fitted into place.

As arranged, Jesse and Bruce met that evening in the bar to exchange notes and swap handouts. Bruce noted that Jesse appeared unusually quiet and reflective. He was obviously brooding about something.

'Did you enjoy the lectures or find them boring?' enquired Bruce.

Jesse paused. 'They certainly weren't boring, but as for enjoying them, well, I don't think that would be quite the right term,' he replied.

Bruce looked puzzled. 'Tell me more,' he said.

'Well,' continued Jesse, 'today has been an enlightenment to me, to say the least. Not only have I learnt about Asperger's Syndrome, but I am now ninety-nine per cent certain that that is what is wrong with my son, Tom.'

'Incredible,' said Bruce and added, 'Let's not be hasty. Let's look at the list of symptoms and characteristics and see how far they correspond with Tom's,' and he took out a relevant sheet from an inside pocket. 'I've got two of these, one for you and one for me.'

Slowly but surely, Jesse and Bruce went through the checklist point by point. Almost every symptom seemed to fit Jesse's lost boy: the relationship problems, the obsessional preoccupation with certain subjects, the failure to read the cues, the inappropriate remarks, the poor eye contact, the good looks. They were all there.

Bruce looked at Jesse. 'You've certainly learnt something today, Jesse,' he said. 'But you're not alone. There are probably a number of people at this conference who are having similar experiences.'

'One of the things which bothers me,' replied Jesse, 'is the fact that so many of us tended to blame or criticise Tom. We regarded his misbehaviour as his fault. It was up to him to pull his socks up and do something about it. We tried to help him but in the end, most of us gave up. Now, of course, I know better. They call it a developmental disorder which the child is born with.'

'For Heaven's sake, Jesse, don't reproach yourself,' said Bruce. 'There are plenty of specialists who have failed to diagnose Asperger's Syndrome, even when it's been right under their nose. It is in fact a condition which has only been highlighted in this country in recent years. We are all learning about it and that's why we are here today. Asperger's Syndrome is one of these hidden conditions. Outwardly the children look absolutely normal, but inwardly they are not. Tourette's Syndrome is another and so is dyslexia. Ideally we need to diagnose these problems as early as possible and then organise appropriate treatment.'

'Yes,' Jesse replied reflectively, as he sipped his glass of beer.

'Well,' he added, 'I must go and phone the wife.'

'So must I,' said Bruce. 'There's a payphone just outside. You go first and I will keep our place here and follow you.'

Jesse soon got through to his wife, Anne. After exchanging pleasantries, she asked him whether he had learnt anything.

'That is an understatement,' Jesse replied.

There was a moment's silence. Anne was a little puzzled.

'Can you remember the subject of the conference?' Jesse continued.

'It was a funny name,' replied Anne, 'something like asparagus?'

'You're almost right,' replied Jesse. 'It's Asperger's Syndrome. It's a German name; the "g" is hard because there are no soft "g"s in German. Anyway, you're a nurse. Here are the symptoms,' he said, referring to his notes. 'Tell me if they remind you of anyone. Number one, relationship problems: these people don't get along with others easily. We know a lot like that, of course. Number two, monomania: from childhood, they have obsessions with subjects such as cars.'

Anne listened carefully.

'Number three, poor eye contact. Number four, inappropriate remarks: they can say embarrassing things in company.'

Anne interrupted. 'You're talking about our Tom.'

'Exactly,' replied Jesse. 'But listen. Number five, good looking. Most of these children are good looking.'

'He certainly was,' said Anne. 'Did he have a real illness that we were ignorant of?' she asked.

'It's called a developmental disorder,' said Jesse, 'and it's not the child's fault. He is born with it.'

By this time Anne felt the tears in her eyes. 'You mean all those years, the poor boy was suffering and we didn't know what was wrong?'

'Exactly,' replied Jesse. 'It's like dyslexia. The teachers and often the parents blame the child for it but it's not their fault. It's how they're made.'

'Can you cure it?' asked Anne.

'It's not an illness like mumps or chickenpox. There's no medicine for it but with the right sort of help, understanding and education, you can help these children to lead relatively normal lives. Apparently, some are very successful. They often have high intelligence and good memories.'

'Tom learnt his tables better than any of our others,' said Anne.

'Well, there you are,' said Jesse, 'but there are a few other points. First, why do you think I'm at this conference?'

'I don't know,' replied Anne.

'I'll tell you. It's because Harry Wilcox talked me into it. He had arranged things before I even knew I was going. It's my belief that he suspected Tom had a problem and he wanted me to learn about it for myself. But that's not all. Apparently, Bruce Whitford who's with me down here reckons that he knows a way to contact Tom. What we do is write a letter to Tom telling him that we don't want to interfere with his life but that we would appreciate it if he could let us know that he is safe and well, and we would be overjoyed if we just had a phone call from him or a letter. We then seal the letter in an envelope with Tom's name on it and we send it to the Salvation Army in London. They have a special bureau for contacting missing people. We give a donation, of course. Bruce will give me the full address on Monday.'

'Anything is worth a try,' said Anne, her voice trembling a little.

'Well, dear, this conference has given us both a lot to think about. I've bought some books on the subject. See you tomorrow. Have a good night.'

'I'll try,' said Anne. 'Goodnight, love.'

Monday morning arrived and the two cleaning ladies, Violet and Iris, were busy cleaning the education office. By half past eight they were emptying the waste baskets in the educational psychologists' department. Arthur Brown, sometimes known as the office jester on account of his frequent practical jokes, was in early as usual and was distributing the post to the various offices. As Violet passed Harry Wilcox's desk, she glanced at his diary for the coming week, which had been left open.

'I see that Dr Wilcox is giving a talk at Duckford,' she used the local term for Duckingford, 'Labour Club on Thursday.'

'Is he?' asked Iris. 'It's a good job that it's not Wednesday. That's Ladies' Night and I understand that they have a male strip show then!'

'The things they get up to these days!' exclaimed Violet.

Arthur's ears pricked up. What an opportunity! he thought with a twinkle in his eye. As the two cleaners disappeared down the corridor, he carefully picked up a rubber, erased the appointment for Thursday on Harry's diary and changed it to Wednesday.

Meanwhile, outside Sockton Infants School, Sarah Craig was busy talking to Mrs Baker and her daughter, Kerry. The idea was to keep Kerry talking to them while she walked into the school. The head teacher had given them special permission to come to the school early. Kelly was quite talkative until she entered the school gates and then, as they feared, her conversation came to an abrupt halt. She certainly was an elective mute in the school situation.

When Bruce arrived in the office that morning, he was surprised to see that Harry Wilcox was already back at work. He had left the door of his room open and was busy at his desk.

'Don't tell me,' Bruce remarked, looking in. 'You discharged yourself from hospital.'

'Not quite,' replied Harry, 'but you're fairly close. I felt that certain authorities considered that I was a little optimistic with regard to my progress. Anyway, I'm back and fairly fit. How did the conference go?'

'Very enlightening,' replied Bruce and added, 'for both Jesse and myself.'

At that moment, Harry and Bruce spied Jesse entering.

'Hello Jesse!' Bruce cried. 'Come and tell Harry what you thought of the conference.'

Harry looked a little uneasy as Jesse advanced. They stared at each other for a moment and then Jesse began, 'I've known you for a long time, Harry, and I was not just a little puzzled about why you wanted me to attend that conference. I now know why. It was a very astute, and I must say, crafty move. You're as crafty as the foxes you chase. You suspected all along that our Tom was a case of Asperger's Syndrome and what better way to enlighten me than to allow me to work it out for myself! Anne and I have talked it over for hours and we are now sure that Tom is a classic case of this condition. In some ways we feel guilty, in other ways, relieved.'

'I must confess,' interrupted Harry, 'that I was not one hundred per cent certain but I knew that you and your wife knew Tom best and as I saw it, the conference provided an excellent opportunity to get us all thinking.'

'I certainly learnt a few things,' added Bruce, and he opened his document case, took out a note and gave it to Jesse. 'These are the details of the address of the Salvation Army department,' he said, and he hurried to his room where the phone was ringing. It was Sarah Craig ringing Bruce to report on the failed attempt to help Kerry Baker, the elective mute.

'It's early days,' said Bruce. 'Please don't give up.'

'I don't intend to,' replied Sarah. 'This is a real challenge. Have you got any ideas?'

'Well,' replied Bruce, 'can you tell me whether Kerry has any favourite toys or hobbies?'

'She's mad about Barbie dolls,' replied Sarah.

'Well, we will buy her a good one and use it as bait. Can we meet for coffee at about three this afternoon in the café on Hill Top?'

'I've got to visit Tanner Park High School first,' replied Sarah. 'I'll do my best.'

As Bruce put the phone down, his eyes settled on a referral letter on the top of his tray. He noted from the address that it was not based in his patch. In fact, it fell in Harry's area, so Bruce picked up the letter and took it immediately to Harry.

'I believe this is one of yours,' said Bruce.

Harry glanced at the name at the top of the letter. 'Oh no,' he groaned, 'not the notorious Parsons family. They have a string of boys as long as my arm. Most of them are rebellious teenagers raging with hormones and misdirected energy. Ah yes, it's Pedro. They got fed up with English names and decided to use an Italian one. At present, Pedro is in a detention centre, another name for the old Borstals, Bruce. They are not fools, the Parsons. My guess is that some of them are intellectually gifted but they're using their abilities in antisocial and criminal ways. I always aim to keep one step ahead of them. Well, it appears to be an urgent case. There's nothing on my timetable for tomorrow as I was still expected to be in convalescence. I will see Pedro tomorrow if they can arrange it.'

During the lunch hour, Bruce slipped out into the town centre. He had already located a toy shop which he had anticipated could be useful for his own children. The one in question had a good selection of Barbie dolls and it didn't take him long to select an unusual one.

'This one has only just come in,' the young shop assistant told him.

Good, thought Bruce, at least there's a fair chance that Kerry Baker did not already have this one.

'I'll take it,' he said. He made sure that he had a detailed receipt of the goods so that he could claim the money back later, since the purchase was related to his work.

The afternoon soon arrived and as arranged, Bruce and Sarah met for coffee in the Hill Top café.

'Did you buy this?' remarked Sarah, handling the doll with interest.

'Yes,' replied Bruce. 'But I hope to be reimbursed by the county since it was purchased in the line of duty or you might say "an indispensable requisite of my job",' he paused and added, 'or yours. The plan, as I see it, would be something like this. First you encourage Kerry to talk about her Barbie dolls on the way to school. A bit of preparation with her mother wouldn't be out of place. Then, as she approaches the danger zone, which in her case appears to be the school gate, you suddenly produce this little surprise,' Bruce pointed to the doll, 'which is still inside the box. You say something like, "Have you seen this Barbie doll, Kerry? Now, if you tell me what you think about this one as we go into school, I may let you keep it, but you must talk to me about what you think, and what you are going to do with her when you take her home, because unless I know what's going to happen to her, I won't let you keep her." Anyway,

Sarah, you get the idea, the aim is to keep the child talking, if possible, through the school playground and into school. It may be a complete flop but we can only try.'

'So,' continued Bruce, 'let's stop talking shop. How's life with you in general?' Bruce recalled that Jesse Fry had told him that Sarah was having problems with her marriage.

Sarah gave him a look which suggested that she was aware that he already knew something.

'Well,' she replied, 'I can't say that my domestic life is the most settled at the moment, but then, whose is? My husband's gone off to the USA. He's been seconded for six months there by his firm. Relationships haven't been good for the past few months, so perhaps the separation will do us both good.' Not wishing to divulge any more, Sarah then enquired how Bruce's house-hunting was going.

'We have our eyes on a property in Hatley,' said Bruce, 'but I'm not building up any hopes because we have got to sell our own house first.'

Sarah looked at Bruce and thought to herself how lucky his wife was to have children and a husband who obviously enjoyed them.

Bruce stared at Sarah, wondering what kind of a man her husband could be to leave such an attractive and intelligent woman. Both could have sat talking for the rest of the afternoon, but work called.

Dr Wilcox's appointment to see Pedro Parsons had been arranged, and accordingly the teenage boy arrived at the education office the next morning, accompanied by two guards. Although a little reticent at first, Pedro adopted a reasonably co-operative attitude in the interview situation. He showed enthusiasm about some of the spatial and constructional tests and, unsurprisingly, made negative comments when Harry enquired about life at the detention centre.

The interview had lasted about twenty-five minutes

He demonstrated enthusiasm with some of the spatial and constructional tests.

when Pedro enquired whether he could be excused to go to the toilet. Harry was a little perturbed, but knowing that the child's custody was the responsibility of the two guards, he showed Pedro where the gents' toilet was, across the corridor, and immediately informed the guards of the boy's whereabouts. By this time, the two guards were busy drinking coffee and chatting to the secretaries.

'As long as we know which room he's in, he's safe enough,' one replied with a smile.

Some five or six minutes passed and Pedro did not return. Harry became a little anxious.

'He's taking a long time,' he called to the guards.

Both guards put their cups down and walked over to the toilets. Pedro was nowhere to be seen. One of the guards noted an open ventilator window. Although it was narrow, Pedro, who was small, nimble and of slight build, would have been quite able to get through such an opening.

'He went out there and legged it,' the guard shouted. 'Quick, outside!'

Once outside the building, the guards had little idea which way to search. First they telephoned the police and then the detention centre. The superintendent at the centre was furious, to say the least, at what he regarded as sheer negligence on the part of his staff. Meanwhile, Harry was back at his desk, adopting as neutral a position as he could. He had made it clear to those around that it was his responsibility to assess the youth's educational and psychological needs, and not to act as his custodian. That was the job of the guards.

That morning another little drama was unfolding at Sockton Infants School. Armed with her newly-purchased Barbie doll, Sarah Craig was walking towards the school playground with Kerry Baker and her mother. The little girl had been encouraged to talk about her favourite toys throughout the journey and Sarah had never seen her so chatty before. She knew that as they approached the school playground, the tension would grow. This was the point at which she should get the child even more engrossed in her subject of Barbie dolls.

'Look!' said Sarah suddenly as she took the box from under her arm. They were almost at the school gate. 'I've got the newest Barbie doll in this box. Do you want to see it?' she asked. 'Do you know her name?'

By this time, they had entered the playground but Kerry appeared oblivious to everything except the existence of the Barbie doll.

'I've read about her,' she said excitedly. 'She's called Annabel.'

'Is she?' replied Sarah. 'Now, what do you think of this idea? If you tell me about your Barbie dolls while we are in the classroom for a few minutes, do you know what I will do? I will let you keep this one for a whole week and if tomorrow we have another chat in the classroom, I'm going to let you keep this Barbie doll for ever and ever, as your very own! Do you like that idea?'

'Yes,' replied Kerry, her eyes lighting up.

'Why do you like this Barbie doll?' asked Sarah.

'Because she's very beautiful,' answered Kerry. By this time, they were in the cloakroom and hanging up Kerry's coat.

The conversation continued down the corridor and into the classroom.

'Where shall we put Annabel?' asked Sarah.

'She will fit in just under my table here,' said Kerry.

As the child was showing Sarah and her mother where the doll could rest during lessons, Miss Hawton, the head teacher, came quietly through the door. To her surprise, she had heard Kerry talking in the corridor and could not resist joining the group. She quietly sidled up to Kerry and said, 'But what about playtime? We can't leave her in here on her own. We must find somewhere safe for her. I've got an idea. When playtime comes, you must ask your teacher if you can take the Barbie doll to my office. Say, "Please, Miss Jones, may I take Annabel to Miss Hawton's office? She said she would look after her for me during playtime." Can you remember that? Now, Kerry, tell me what you are going to say to Miss Jones.'

Kerry repeated the instruction, word for word. The three adults were delighted. It was decided that the achievement should not be pushed any further. Kerry Baker, who had been an elective mute in the school situation for over two years, had at last demonstrated that her problem could be overcome. She had had her first conversation with her head teacher.

Having made a call at one of the local schools, it was mid-morning by the time Bruce Whitford arrived at the office. The subject of Pedro Parsons's escape through the lavatory window was still the centre of discussion. Meeting Bruce in the office, Harry Wilcox relayed the story to him.

'He asked to be excused. I watched him go into the gents' in the corridor. I informed the guards, and after that it was surely their responsibility,' proclaimed Harry.

Bruce could not help but appreciate the amusing part of the situation and with his tongue in his cheek, remarked, 'As you said yesterday, Harry, it's always necessary to be one step ahead of the Parsons.'

'True,' replied Harry, trying to appear totally oblivious to any veiled criticism which may, or may not, have been implied by the remark. 'Well, I have a lecture to prepare now. According to my diary, I'm due to give a talk on child development to the Young Wives' Association at the Duckingford Labour Club tomorrow night,' and he disappeared into his office.

Bruce was busy going through his post when someone knocked on his office door. It was Sarah Craig, fresh from her success at Sockton Infants School. She was beaming with triumph and Bruce could not help but feel that she was going to give him some good news.

'Well,' he queried, 'don't tell me it failed again?'

'Not at all,' replied Sarah, as she drew breath and sat on the chair before him. 'It went like a bomb. The Barbie doll was the key to success. We kept Kerry talking all the way down the road, through the gate and across the school playground and, would you believe it, into the school and down the corridor. She was still chatting inside the classroom. In fact, Miss Hawton, the head teacher, came into the classroom while all this was going on and she actually spoke to her. You've never seen anything like the relief on Mrs Baker's face when she left the school. She was jubilant.

'But,' continued Sarah, 'there's a follow-up to this. At playtime it was agreed that Kerry should take the Barbie doll to Miss Hawton's office, to be looked after there during the break. Her task was to ask Miss Hawton to do this. Shall I ring and see if she did?' Sarah asked excitedly. She then paused and added, 'Better still, you ring. After all, it was your idea.'

'One thing to have an idea, another to implement it successfully,' said Bruce as he picked up the phone.

Sarah watched him intently as the conversation between Bruce and Miss Hawton ensued.

'She did wonderfully well,' he repeated. 'Of course the test is going to be to continue this tomorrow and thereafter. Do you think we could extend this idea of Kerry's interest in Barbie dolls by inviting her to bring one of her own on certain days to show her teacher, who could encourage her to discuss it and, as today, she could leave it with you at playtime in order to encourage further conversation in the classroom? The secret in overcoming elective mutism is perpetuating the initial success.'

When Bruce placed the receiver back on the phone, he

and Sarah stared at each other for a few moments in mutual admiration.

'This really calls for a celebration,' he said and then, impulsively and with an unsteady and subdued voice, added, 'Are you free tomorrow night for a quiet drink?'

'Of course I am,' Sarah replied. 'I'm free every night now.'

'Well, you know the area better than I do,' Bruce went on. 'Do you know a quiet place in the country where two friends could have a quiet and discreet drink?'

'I know just the place,' replied Sarah. 'What about a bar meal thrown in?'

'Excellent,' said Bruce.

'It's called the Prince Regent,' Sarah continued. 'It's in a tiny, picturesque village called Prince Common in the north of the county. I can get there by half past seven and if you happen to be there as well, what a coincidence it will be!'

By putting it this way, she felt that any guilt which either may have felt in making the date was to some extent reduced, and Bruce certainly approved.

By half past seven on Wednesday evening, women from various parts of the county were converging on Duckingford Labour Club. The car park was filling up and at one point a coach unloaded around forty lively female passengers from a nearby town. Ladies' Night at the club had become very popular. The big feature was the male strip show. Doris Dicker, accompanied by a friend, was among the crowd. It would be a change from wrestling, she had imagined.

As Harry Wilcox drew up in the car park, he was pleased to see that his talk was attracting such a large audience. Was it his natural charisma or the subject of the talk which was the attraction? Probably a combination of both, he mused.

Once in the building, Harry soon located an inner office. Two club administrators, the manager and his secretary, were sitting behind a desk. Both were dressed in bow ties and evening suits.

'The name's Wilcox, Dr Wilcox, I've come to entertain the ladies of Duckingford,' Harry announced with a beam.

A smartly-dressed middle-aged man was not quite what the staff were expecting but they had left the bookings to an agency and, not wishing to appear rude, one replied, 'Oh, yes. Well, I will show you to your room and if you could be ready in a quarter of an hour, we will then give you a shout.'

This was unusual, thought Harry, but very nice to be offered a quiet place to prepare oneself for the evening's talk.

Accordingly, the club secretary took Harry to a small room just off the stage. 'What did you say your name was?' he asked.

'Dr Harry Wilcox,' replied Harry.

'I'll remember that,' said the secretary and leaving Harry in the dressing room, he returned to the office.

'He's certainly different,' the club secretary said to his manager. His stage name is Dr Harry Wilcox. I wonder what he's hiding in the document case.'

'I wondered about that myself,' his colleague replied. You certainly get some oddbods here on Wednesdays.'

He had hardly finished talking when a strapping young man with long hair and what appeared to be a skin-tight silk sweatsuit of many colours appeared at the door. 'I'm doing a floor show tonight for the ladies,' he announced.

'Another one,' remarked the secretary.

'Oh,' replied the young man, 'have I got a rival? Can I go on last?'

'Certainly,' replied the manager and escorted him to another room just off the stage.

Meanwhile, in the adjacent dressing room, Harry Wilcox was admiring himself in the mirror, straightening his tie and practising his introduction. 'Thank you, madam chairperson,' the title 'madam chairperson' often got a laugh, he thought, 'and good evening, ladies.'

Hardly had Harry finished muttering to himself when the door opened and the secretary once again appeared.

'Are you ready, Dr Wilcox?'

'Raring to go,' replied Harry with a grin.

'Follow me,' instructed the secretary. He pointed to the stage curtains. 'I will go on first and announce you. When you hear the applause, I shall disappear off the other side of the stage, and then you come on.'

Extraordinary, thought Harry. But why shouldn't an introduction be different? Accordingly, he paused and waited as the secretary brushed through the curtains.

'Ladies,' he heard him shout. 'An outstanding surprise for you tonight. A man with a difference.'

'I hope it's a big one!' a young lady shouted from the front row.

The secretary paused and grinned. 'Who knows?' he went on. 'Here he is, the Man of the Moment, Dr Harry Wilcox.'

Doris Dicker sitting near the back of the hall gasped. She could hardly believe her ears.

A small three-piece band struck up and the audience burst into a crescendo as Harry, complete with document case and a huge beam on his face, appeared on the stage. For a brief few seconds, a hush fell over the hall. Harry looked disconcerted. There was no table on which to rest his document case, full of visual aids and transparencies with which he normally embellished his talks, and not even a chair to sit on.

Harry looked at the audience which seemed to consist of numerous tightly-knit groups gathered around small tables, most of which were covered with glasses and bottles of drink.

'Has anyone a spare table?' Harry asked as politely as he could. 'And a chair if possible?' he added.

'You can have this one,' a lady shouted. 'We can double up with our friends.' By this time the audience had decided that the request was all part of the showman's routine. The table, complete with a chair, was soon lifted on to the stage.

'Is there an overhead projector?' Harry asked.

The ladies began to chuckle and one yelled out, 'If you stand on the table, we can then see your overhead projector!'

Harry smiled, a little uncertain of the implication of the statement. The audience roared. Tension was mounting. What kind of treat were they expecting? By this time, he had deduced that he would have to deliver his talk without the usual visual aids. He had always prided himself on his versatility and adaptability, and over the years he had made use of a number of opening gambits. Placing his document case on the table before him, he began, 'Now ladies, I want you to feel completely at ease. Don't be afraid to ask any questions you like.' Harry always claimed to be prepared to deal with 'the rabbit punch', as he called the sort of question which was always designed to knock him off balance. At his best, he was also capable of wit, parody and pure burlesque. He went on, 'I always say that a good talk is like a woman's dress: long enough to cover the subject but short enough to retain interest.'

He paused, expecting at least an appreciative chuckle but none came, and then from the back of the hall, Doris Dicker, who could no longer contain herself, piped up, 'Get your dress off, we're waiting.'

Thinking that there was a drunk or deranged idiot in the audience and determined to ignore her, Harry paused and continued, 'As a psychologist, I often find that it is useful to stick to the bare facts.'

By this time, the audience were getting uneasy and agitated. 'Let's see your bare facts,' one frustrated customer bellowed.

'Get 'em off,' another roared.

Harry was determined not to give in and he told his audience just that. 'Ladies,' he shouted. 'A man who gives in when he's wrong is wise, but a man who gives in when he's right, is married, and, ladies, I am not married,' he added with a smirk.

'I thought so, he's one of those,' shouted a middle-aged mother, brandishing a glass.

'I have come here tonight,' Harry raised his voice, 'to deliver a lecture.'

'On what?' someone shouted.

'On how to bring up children.'

'How do you know? You're not married,' shouted another female.

'Maybe he's got children but he is not married,' ventured her drinking companion.

Still determined to continue with his talk, Harry went on. 'Nobody likes change but a wet baby.'

'We're waiting for you to change, let's have the bare facts,' someone jeered. 'Strip off!' The cry seemed to be taken up repeatedly by everyone in the hall.

By this time even Harry's patience was exhausted.

'I find this whole atmosphere intellectually insulting and morally repugnant,' Harry yelled above the pandemonium and with that, he picked up his document case and stalked off the stage. Passing the manager on his way out, he remarked, 'I have never come across such an uncouth rabble. Please don't ever invite me here again.'

The manager looked perplexed as he watched Harry depart from the building.

Meanwhile, out in the rural north of the county, Bruce had arrived at the Prince Regent in Prince Common. It was an olde-worlde-style inn dating back to Tudor times. It was popular with the locals and those from farther afield. By the time Bruce arrived, most of the tables were occupied. He had not noticed Sarah's car in the car park and noting the popularity of the place, he quickly ordered a drink and found a table suitable for two in a small alcove. He had hardly settled down when Sarah arrived. 'It's filling up already,' she remarked.

'What's your poison?' asked Bruce, smiling.

'A shandy, I think,' replied Sarah.

They were soon engrossed in conversation. The subject ranged from the pubs they had visited in the past to family affairs and Bruce's progress in house-hunting, work inevitably, and Harry Wilcox's personality.

'I understand that Harry is giving a talk to the Duckingford Young Wives at the Labour Club tonight,' remarked Bruce.

'Is he?' replied Sarah. 'Wednesday night, as far as I know, is Ladies' Night over there and the last thing they want is a talk on child psychology. In fact I've heard that the club has a male strip show on Wednesdays and it attracts women from all over the county. It's quite a moneyspinner and a lot of drink is sold. The Labour Club makes a lot of money on Wednesdays.'

Hearing this, Bruce chuckled. 'Are you thinking what I'm thinking?'

'Yes,' replied Sarah. 'But I can't imagine Harry Wilcox being tricked into doing a striptease. In fact, I could imagine you doing it rather than Harry,' she grinned mischievously.

Just then two girls who were collecting empty glasses came near the alcove and both Sarah and Bruce could not fail to hear the remark made by one of them: 'He's been belting those children again. If he goes on, I shall inform the police,' one said.

'The brute,' the other remarked.

The screams of terrified children were coming from the room.

Bruce and Sarah looked at each other but said nothing.

'I'll go and get another drink,' said Bruce.

'Please don't,' replied Sarah. 'It's my turn – I've got to go to the car quickly.' Sarah had realised that she had left her handbag on the seat in her car. No sooner was she outside the door, than she came running back. 'Bruce, can you come outside?' she asked him anxiously.

Within seconds they were both in the car park. Sarah pointed to an upstairs window where a light was on. The screams of terrified children were coming from the room.

'Please, don't, Daddy!' a girl could be heard shouting.

Both Sarah and Bruce felt cold and sickened by the sheer terror of the children's screams.

'What can we do?' said Sarah. They both realised the implications of becoming involved formally. It would hardly be discreet if their date became public knowledge.

'I now understand what that barmaid meant,' said Bruce.

Sarah nodded and then added, 'These children are obviously vulnerable. This is not the first time. It's our duty to do something. The head teacher of the local school, Amy Chalk, she's a bit of a gossip – some call her "Chalk and Talk", is a friend of mine. It's likely that these children go to Prince Common Primary. I will ring her up and say that a friend of mine is suspicious that the children of the pub landlord are being battered. In that way, you certainly won't be involved. I will do that tomorrow and we can play it from there. The county has a set procedure for child battering cases. If it's serious, the Social Services or possibly the NSPCC would be alerted.'

'Do you want another drink?' Bruce asked.

'Not in there,' replied Sarah, 'and it's a bit late to go anywhere else,' she added.

A few moments of embarrassing silence followed, during which each one waited for the other to make a suggestion. Then Bruce blurted out, 'Well, I enjoyed tonight up until this business.' He gesticulated towards the window where the noise had now subsided. 'I suppose we must make our separate ways. See you tomorrow.'

'Take care,' called Sarah as she opened her car door.

Despite his unfortunate experiences of the previous evening, Harry was remarkably placid the next morning. This was fortunate, since his first case, an eight-year-old boy suffering from hyperactivity, was already squirming in his seat in the waiting room with his mother. Harry introduced himself to the boy and his mother and then took the child to his room, where he gave him a series of ability tests. The child's co-operation and attention were not easily enlisted but, making use of his professional expertise and years of experience, Harry managed to interest the child enough to establish that he was at least of normal intelligence, if under-achieving in certain scholastic subjects, such as reading and spelling. From time to time, the youngster, being easily distracted, had to be stopped from handling various objects on Harry's desk or looking around at other items of interest associated with his job. He was also constantly asking questions.

'What's your name?' he asked.

'Dr Wilcox,' Harry replied.

The boy looked at Harry incredulously. 'I don't want to see a doctor! I don't want medicine,' he protested.

'I'm not that sort of doctor,' said Harry. 'I'm trying to find out how clever you are and as far as I can see, you're quite clever.'

The boy reached for Harry's stopwatch. 'Don't touch that,' said Harry, raising his voice a little. 'Let's see if you can make this pattern with these blocks.' The boy's interest was easily aroused.

Meanwhile, in an adjacent room, Sarah Craig had rung her friend, Amy Chalk, the headmistress of Prince Common Primary School. 'Amy,' she said, 'I wonder if you could give us some information on the family who run the Prince Regent pub in your village. A friend of mine visited the pub last night and it appears that there is some evidence that the children are being battered.'

Amy paused. 'The new landlord,' she confided, 'is called Rutter. I've heard that he is a bit of a "rotter". Excuse the pun. The family came from the north. They have been here about four months. There are three children, all girls, and they are all at this school. Jenny is the eldest. She's an intelligent and pretty girl. All three seem rather cowed and attached to their teachers. I can see Jenny at this moment in the playground by coincidence. Her class is doing PE and she is the only one who is wearing a woollen jumper. The rest are in vests and shorts. I wonder why... I'll tell you what, I will go out and have a quiet talk with her teacher and see if I can learn anything, and then I will ring you back.'

Later that morning Amy Chalk was on the phone again to Sarah Craig. She had learnt from Jenny Rutter's teacher that the child had refused to take off her jumper, saying that it was too cold. However, when Amy Chalk had taken the child to her study and insisted that she took it off, it was discovered that the child was covered in bruises. Amy knew the county procedure for such incidents and had immediately phoned the doctor and the Social Services Department, who within a short time had visited the school, and photographs of the child's bruises had been taken as evidence. The doctor said that there was also linear bruising in both the umbilical and buttocks regions, which was probably done by a cane or stick.

'Perhaps the NSPCC should be involved as well,' suggested Sarah. Cases of child battering were always difficult to deal with. If a child was placed in care, it could herald the start of a process which might end with the break-up of the whole family. Tact and diplomacy were often required in handling the parents, and also firmness in order to try to protect the child from future assaults. As Sarah put down the phone, she felt some relief. At least the right authorities were now in charge.

By the time Sarah had completed her phone call, Harry Wilcox was engaged in a counselling session with Miss Woodcock, the mother of Paul, the hyperactive child.

'Well,' said Harry, drawing his breath and deliberately taking his time, 'Paul seems to be like a racing car. Good body, good motor,' Harry pointed to his cranium, indicating the home of the brain, 'but unfortunately, no brakes!'

Miss Woodcock continued to stare at Harry as he continued.

'Paul is what is sometimes known as a hyperactive child with problems in sustaining attention. I have a checklist of symptoms, or characteristics, of these children. I wonder if you could tell me whether they apply to Paul?'

'One: has difficulty in remaining seated?'

'Yes,' replied Miss Woodcock.

'He certainly did with me,' added Harry.

'Two: often fidgets with hands and feet or squirms on a seat?'

'Yes,' replied Miss Woodcock again.

'I found that as well,' said Harry.

'Three: has difficulty in awaiting turns?'

'Yes,' Miss Woodcock again replied.

'Four: talks excessively?'

'Never stops,' said Miss Woodcock and they both heard Paul who, at that moment, was busy asking a secretary in the office how her typewriter worked.

By the time Harry had reached number fourteen on the checklist, he had concluded that Paul was a classic case of what the Americans termed 'ADHD' which stood for Attention Deficit/Hyperactivity Disorder.

'Yes, I thought as much,' Harry concluded. 'Paul has

ADHD or Attention Deficit/Hyperactivity Disorder.'

Miss Woodcock was completely bemused. For a moment she stared at Harry and then blurted out. 'I don't care what you call it. My child needs help.'

Bruce found no shortage of news and activity when he arrived back at the office. Like many offices, there was a very good bush telegraph and details of Harry Wilcox's abortive visit to the Duckingford Labour Club had soon been circulated and generally enjoyed by the staff. Bruce had hardly closed the door of his room and sat at his desk when he was visited by Sarah Craig. She quickly enlightened Bruce about Harry's escapade the previous evening and then about the information she had gleaned from Amy Chalk regarding the case of the child battering at the Prince Regent pub in Prince Common.

Bruce listened intently. 'It seems to be a case for Social Services and the police,' he concluded. 'Thanks for keeping my name out of it, Sarah.'

'I've done my best to keep both of our names out of it,' she replied. 'Anyway, I've got an appointment at the other end of the borough. Must love you and leave you,' and with that, she left the office.

For a few moments, Bruce pondered on Sarah's final statement. Was it just a spur of the moment statement? Was there any significance? Bruce had been married for seven years and suddenly the saying, 'the seven year itch' came to his mind.

Chapter Six
A Boxing Tournament

It was over a month later, in early November, when Jesse Fry and his wife, Anne, received a phone call from the Missing Persons Bureau of the Salvation Army. The news was positive. The officer on the end of the line was able to inform them that their letter had been delivered to their wayward son and that he was alive and well. In keeping with the code of strict confidentiality, however, no other information regarding Tom's activities or occupation could be divulged to them.

By means of computer records of employment registration numbers, the Salvation Army had located Tom in the dockyard in Portsmouth and an officer had delivered his parents' letter to him one morning as he was lowered by pulley from the side of a ship which he had been painting. His reaction had been mixed. An individual who suffers from the condition known as Asperger's Syndrome does not perceive life in the same way as other people. Through no fault of their own, individuals with this disorder are largely lacking in empathy or the ability to stand in another's shoes. Feelings of guilt or remorse can be conveniently pushed aside and blame is automatically and easily projected on others. And so it was with Tom. Having read the letter, he stuffed it in the pocket of his overalls and pushed it into the back of his mind.

Tom considered that his way of perceiving the world

An officer had delivered his parents' letter to him one morning as he was lowered by pulley from the side of a ship he had been painting.

was the right one and those who did not fall in line with his perceptions were wrong or misguided. It has been said that the difference between a neurotic and a psychotic is that a neurotic has a problem and knows it whilst a psychotic has a problem but is unaware of it. Asperger's Syndrome would appear to be more of a psychosis than a neurosis. When this aspect of the condition is appreciated, the difficulty in trying to help such individuals can be realised. Far more than normal counselling is required. Like most disorders, however, there are varying degrees of the problem. At the heart of the Asperger condition is an awkwardness with social relationships, and that is why individuals with the problem often succeed in employment or work where social interaction is minimal. Tom had tried many jobs since leaving home but most had failed on account of relationship problems. Painting the sides of ships, though dangerous, was well paid, exciting and did not require a lot of human interaction. For the present it suited him.

On hearing the news that their son was alive and well, both Jesse and Anne Fry experienced a great sense of relief and the following day Jesse conveyed the news to Bruce Whitford when they met in the car park of the Town Hall.

'Thanks to your idea and the Sally Army, we at least now know that he's alive,' Jesse told Bruce.

'I'm delighted,' replied Bruce, who at that time was grappling with personal problems of his own, not least of which was the fact that the chain involved in the selling of their house was on the point of collapse. Relationships with Sarah Craig were also beginning to bother him. What originally had begun as an apparently carefree friendship, had slowly drifted into an emotional tangle. The danger signals had become apparent to both and neither knew how to handle them.

At least someone is happy today, thought Bruce to himself as he drove away to his next appointment which was with a nine-year-old boy who had been referred to him for handwriting difficulties. The school which the boy attended was Barley Primary, located in the village of the same name on the edge of Monaston.

Within twenty minutes, Bruce had arrived at the school and was setting up his testing material in the school library. He always commenced his testing session with a rough screening measure for colour-blindness. This was a test which was normally carried out by the Health Department but owing to a shortage of staff some children escaped the net and Bruce soon discovered that Georgie Potopowicz, the nine-year-old boy he was presently testing, was one of those. There was no evidence in his case notes of colour-blindness. Bruce quickly looked outside the interview room where the child's mother was sitting on a chair in the corridor.

'Did you know that Georgie appears to be colour-blind?' he asked Mrs Potopowicz.

She looked at him questioningly and then replied, 'Oh, perhaps that's why he doesn't like playing Ludo.'

'I don't think I would, if I couldn't see the difference between colours,' added Bruce. 'Anyway, we will discuss it later,' and he returned to the assessment.

Although he appeared to be relatively intelligent, Georgie had great difficulty in writing or manipulating a pencil. Bruce did a whole series of laterality tests on the child. He discovered that Georgie liked looking through his left eye, listening to the ticking of a stopwatch through his left ear and kicking a rolled-up piece of paper with his left foot. When asked to cut some paper, Georgie promptly picked up the scissors in his left hand and made a crude attempt at cutting along a line on the paper. Next Bruce gave the child a ball and asked him to throw it back to him. Again Georgie carried out the activity with his left hand. By this time Bruce had concluded that he was probably dealing with a 'shifted sinistral' or 'shifted left-hander' and that this might well explain the child's poor handwriting.

Bruce next tested Georgie's intelligence and, having completed some further scholastic attainment tests in reading, spelling and arithmetic, Bruce took the child back to his classroom. By this time it was mid-morning break and Georgie's teacher was able to join Bruce and the child's mother in the interview room.

'That was a very interesting session,' Bruce began. 'First we found that Georgie is colour-blind, didn't we, Mrs Potopowicz?'

'Yes,' replied Georgie's mother and added, 'I do believe that his grandfather, my father, is also colour-blind. He wanted to fly aeroplanes during the war but he wasn't allowed to because of his colour-blindness.'

'That doesn't surprise me,' said Bruce. 'Colour-blindness often runs in families and normally only affects males. The women are the carriers. They carry the genes of colour-blindness but they are not affected. Well, first I would like to say,' he explained, 'that colour-blindness is a problem which we need to be aware of, but it is not that serious and I'm afraid there is no cure for it. I'm going to give you a copy of these guidance notes, Mrs Potopowicz. You can read them when you go home. You will see that there are a few careers which colour-blind people cannot go into because it could be dangerous, for example some jobs in the Services or the police, jobs to do with electrical fitting, and so on. Electric wires are often coloured and if you got them mixed up it could cause trouble, couldn't it? In school when Georgie is colouring or doing painting, the teacher should be aware that he doesn't see colours the same way as other children, and there are some colours which he doesn't see at all. Later on when he comes to do his GCSE in Geography he must be given special consideration with regard to coloured maps. Map-reading isn't easy when you can't tell red from green.'

Both Georgie's teacher and his mother were intrigued.

'Now,' continued Bruce, 'the reason I was asked to see Georgie in the first place was because of his poor handwriting. What I have found out about Georgie is that he prefers to do a lot of things with the left side of his body. He kicks with his left foot, he puts a kaleidoscope up to his left eye, he listens to the ticking of a stopwatch with his left ear and he even throws a ball with his left hand. Tell me, Mrs Potopowicz, does he switch a knife and fork when eating?'

'He tries to, but his grandfather won't let him,' replied Mrs Potopowicz, and she went on, 'When he was young, he even tried to write with his left hand but his grandfather said that it was a right-handed world and he must write with his right hand.'

'Did he ever have any problems with his speech when he was young?' Bruce asked.

She replied, 'He used to stutter a bit but he now seems to have grown out of it.'

Bruce reflected and then said, 'I think I understand Georgie's problem. He's what is known as a "shifted sinistral" or "shifted left-hander". It could be that he has been made to write with his right hand when he is really a left-hander and hence he finds it difficult. He just can't get the pressure right for writing and hence he is a poor handwriter. This is nothing new but it's unfortunate and in some ways the whole business is bound up with religion and race.'

Bruce reflected on Georgie's surname. 'Is your husband Polish?' he asked.

'Yes,' replied Mrs Potopowicz.

'And is he Roman Catholic?'

'Yes,' replied Mrs Potopowicz again.

'You see,' went on Bruce, 'if you read the Bible, you

may have heard about the sheep and the goats. The good people will stand on the right of the Lord and the bad on the left. Down through the ages, this has been taken literally and misinterpreted. We hear that things will be all right, not "all left". We hear about the righteous, not the "lefteous".

'In the Middle Ages, if you had red hair or three nipples or were left-handed, you were sometimes regarded as a witch and could be burnt at the stake. The left-handers have been given a poor deal down through the ages. People say it's a right-handed world but it's only what Man has made it into. If you go to Australia, you will find that nearly forty per cent of Aborigines are left-handed. They have special left-handed boomerangs. In Africa there are whole tribes who are left-handed. When a child is left-handed, he should be allowed to be so. He should be allowed to switch a knife and fork or use a spoon with his left hand.

'Some of the cleverest people in the world are left-handed. Some recent research shows that there is a higher percentage of high intelligence in the left-handed population as opposed to the right.' Bruce paused for a moment and then said, 'I won't go on any more about the subject. Sinistrality, or left-handedness, is one of my hobbyhorses, but what I am trying to say is that your son, Georgie, may well be naturally left-handed and since he has been made to write with his right hand he has poor handwriting. Because he is now used to writing with his right hand and there are some advantages in doing so, I don't think it would be wise to encourage him to use his left hand to write. However, it is important to remember that when it comes to writing, Georgie should be given extra time and special consideration. When he comes to take examinations, when he is much older, of course, and if he is still having problems with handwriting, he will be eligible for what we call a special dispensationary certificate which will allow him extra time to do his exams and he won't be penalised or marked down for poor handwriting.

'Meanwhile, here is a booklet,' Bruce handed Georgie's teacher a thin book. 'It contains suggestions for teachers and parents to help encourage a child to adopt a more effective handwriting posture and pencil grip. In Georgie's case I would suggest that he holds the pencil a little further away from the nib because at the moment he is obscuring his work as he completes it. It may be that he will find a three-sided pencil like this very useful,' Bruce picked up a pencil he had near him, 'as it should help him to develop a better tripod grip,' and he demonstrated the appropriate hold.

'Finally, watch Georgie's non-writing hand. He is rather lazy with it. He lets it dangle by his side when he should use it more effectively to balance the paper. I'll try to look in again in a few weeks to see how Georgie is doing,' and Bruce brought the interview session to an end.

Within a short time Bruce was back in his office at the Town Hall. He had hardly begun to go through his in-tray when Harry appeared at his door, accompanied by a well-dressed Indian gentleman.

'Bruce,' exclaimed Harry, 'let me introduce you to my good friend, Dr Harjit Patel.'

Bruce stood and shook hands with a tall, good-looking gentleman of obvious Indian extraction.

'Harjit,' continued Harry, 'has a particular interest in Riding for the Disabled. Have you heard of it?' asked Harry.

'I think so,' said Bruce, a little unsure, 'but tell me more.'

'Well,' went on Harry, 'the Riding for the Disabled Association has groups right across the country, in fact across Europe. It is based on the idea that disabled people and particularly children – and this applies to both the mentally and physically handicapped – not only enjoy horse-riding but also that it helps their co-ordination and self-confidence.'

At this point Dr Patel joined in. 'Yes,' he said, 'with hemiplegics, for instance, four strong legs take the place of two weak ones. It's a strange thing,' he continued. 'When the horses have physically or mentally-handicapped children or adults riding them they seem to sense it. They kind of empathise with them.'

'Oh, I think horse-riding can be a wonderful therapy,' added Bruce, 'and even for maladjusted children.'

'That's right,' said Dr Patel, smiling with obvious pleasure at Bruce's apparently positive response. 'Do you know that it can help to get school refusal children out of the home and build up their self-image? Horse-riding can help in all sorts of ways. We even had one case of a child with expressive aphasia – you know, no speech – and he uttered his first words to his horse.'

'Did the horse reply?' asked Bruce facetiously, whereupon Harry could not help but interject with the word 'Neigh'.

Having recovered from the temporary hilarity, Harry went on to explain that Harjit Patel was the real inspiration behind the idea for an equestrian centre and was pivotal in its creation. He himself had formed a committee with the long-term aim of raising enough money to build an equestrian centre on the outskirts of Monaston. The centre was to offer facilities for both the able-bodied and the disabled. The committee had already earmarked some appropriate land for the site of the centre. The land in question belonged to the local authority, and with the support of the council could be rented at a fair rate.

Harjit Patel, who could be quite manipulative when he wished, had used his influence as a local medical practitioner to enlist support for the scheme from representatives of both political parties.

'In this way you can't lose,' he exclaimed. 'Both sides like to be seen as helping the handicapped. It improves their image in the locality.'

'Well, those are our long-term aims,' explained Harry. 'Every so often we run projects or events to raise money and our next one is a big boxing tournament at the Duckingford Town Hall this Friday. Are you going to support us, Bruce?'

'Of course,' replied Bruce. 'My wife is coming out again this weekend. Can she come too?'

'Support means not only buying your own ticket but selling some if you can on your round,' Harry continued.

'I can only try,' said Bruce, 'although I wouldn't make the salesman that you would, Harry.' They exchanged smiles.

'Who are the boxers who will be competing in the tournament?' Bruce asked.

'Oh, we have a number of very good local boys,' answered Harry. 'But the star attraction is an exhibition bout given by Freddie Barnes who, as you know, was once the Middleweight Champion of the World.'

'I remember his name from years ago,' said Bruce, surprised. 'Is he still boxing?'

'Oh, yes, but only friendly exhibition matches,' Harry replied.

'Well, you have certainly got a big name there to draw the crowd,' Bruce remarked.

'We have had a few big names in support of the equestrian centre,' Harry went on. 'Another is the comedian, Benny Gayton. He gives us a lot of support.'

'Benny Gayton!' exclaimed Bruce.

'That's right. He was brought up in Monaston and still has a house here, lives with his mother,' Harry continued. 'When he comes along to one of our functions he is usually accompanied by a couple of his bodyguards.' Harry grinned.

'I can believe it,' said Bruce. 'He's very popular on television.'

'Well, to make the boxing tournament more entertaining, we have asked Benny to act as the referee and he has agreed as long as he can have his bodyguards nearby in case things become a little rough.'

'That should be a crowd-puller,' said Bruce.

'We've already sold a lot of tickets,' replied Harry. 'There will be the usual raffles of course and important guests like yourself will be invited to a small buffet before the action begins.'

At that moment, Harry's secretary looked into the room to inform him that he was needed on the phone. Bruce had hardly settled down to go through his post when his own phone rang. It was his wife, Marie. He could tell from her tone that the news was not good, and he sensed correctly. The sale of their house, which at one time appeared to be proceeding smoothly, had fallen through. Bruce did his best to cheer up his wife and mentioned that he had arranged for them to go to a surprise event, the boxing tournament, that coming Friday when she was due to visit Monaston again.

Having read his correspondence and dictated some letters to his secretary, Bruce picked up the details of his next appointment which he noted was a nine-year-old boy at Goose Common Middle School. He left in a hurry. He would read the details of the referral when he arrived at the school.

The drive took about twenty minutes and as Bruce arrived in the staff car park the children were filing in for their afternoon lessons. As was the custom for any school appointment, Bruce went straight to the head teacher's office and knocked on the door.

'Come in,' shouted Doug Brown, the head teacher, who was always smartly dressed and every inch the professional.

'I've come to see Tim Potter,' said Bruce politely.

'Ah, yes. Well, no doubt you've read the history. We are just wondering whether Tim is best placed in a normal school.'

Bruce did not say that he had not prepared himself with the papers.

'I'm teaching until break time,' continued Doug, 'so you are welcome to use this room. Make yourself at home and I will send Tim along.'

Bruce had hardly had time to clear the desk and set up his testing material when a knock came at the door.

'Come in,' called Bruce.

The door opened and a well-built little boy with dark hair, rosy cheeks and a bright smile literally hopped in.

'I'm Tim Potter,' he exclaimed.

Bruce could not hold back his surprise as he immediately recognised the child's problem. He only had one leg.

The little boy grinned at Bruce and added, 'I'm what they call an amputee. I had an argument with a ten-ton truck on the A5 and lost a leg.'

What a brave child! thought Bruce, trying to collect his thoughts together and searching for something appropriate to say. Eventually he said, 'Well, Tim, you seem to be full of life. I'm going to give you some tests and I've got a feeling that you're going to enjoy them.'

'I like tests,' replied Tim in eager anticipation, and he soon became engrossed in the various test items. It did not take long for Bruce to establish that Tim was a child of above-average intelligence and scholastic attainments to match. The reason for assessing Tim was not so much one of establishing his ability but rather to ascertain whether he was appropriately placed in a normal school situation or whether he should be offered a place in a special school for

Tim watched him hop speedily across the playground.

physically-handicapped children.

After the testing session Bruce chatted with Tim, who informed him that he liked his present school and had a number of good friends there. He managed to participate in most of the school activities and even did some athletics. In the high jump, for instance, Tim had learnt how to dive over the bar and had attained greater heights than some children who jumped in the normal fashion. After the interview, Bruce bade farewell to Tim. As he watched him hop speedily across the playground, the biblical quotation *Suffer the little children* came naturally to his mind.

Within minutes Doug Brown and the child's parents joined him.

Doug introduced Bruce to Mr and Mrs Potter and as he shook hands with them, he sensed some anxiety or nervousness in their manner. 'What a delightful, little boy you have!' commenced Bruce. 'An example to us all, don't you think?'

'We think the world of him,' replied Mr Potter.

'I can understand that,' continued Bruce, 'and academically you probably already know that he falls well into the above average range.'

'He does?' questioned Tim's mother and with that, Doug Brown, the headmaster broke in.

'You see, Mr Whitford, for a long time I've been trying to reassure Mr and Mrs Potter that Tim is perfectly well integrated here. He is a popular boy and participates in most of the normal school activities.'

'So I understand,' replied Bruce. 'There is one point, however. I believe that Tim is due to be fitted with an artificial leg in the near future. If this is the case, it may be in his interests to spend a short time at a school for physically-handicapped children where he will receive physiotherapy and specialist help from experts in artificial limbs. I will look into that. But I see no reason why Tim cannot be educated for most of his school career in a normal school like this one. It may be that he could be visited here by a specialist, or at home. I will enquire about the matter. Are you happy with that, Mr and Mrs Potter?'

Tim's parents appeared reasonably satisfied with the arrangements and the interview came to a close.

Friday soon arrived and as Bruce drove back from an afternoon appointment on that day his mind was on the activities of the forthcoming evening. He was due to pick up Marie from the station at six o'clock. They could then go quickly to the boarding house where he was staying, wash and change and then head off to Duckingford Town Hall where they had been invited for a buffet meal before watching the boxing tournament. The evening promised to be an interesting one with the celebrities, Benny Gayton and Freddie Barnes.

On arriving at the car park of the Council House, Bruce met Harry carrying his document case and in an obvious hurry.

'Can't stop,' he called to Bruce, 'I'm already late. I've got to go to Duckingford to prepare for tonight's proceedings. Looking forward to seeing you and your wife at the buffet tonight.'

'About seven o'clock,' replied Bruce.

'That's right,' shouted Harry as he jumped in his car and drove off.

The train was on time and Bruce met Marie at the station as planned. Marie was bursting with news as they drove to the boarding house and it was not all good. The situation with regard to selling their house had improved. A firm offer had been made by a young couple who were first-time buyers, who had also made a fair offer for the carpets; also Bruce's second child was not too happy to have a brace fitted over her teeth; problems had occurred with the central heating and it appeared that a sizeable bill was in the offing. Finally, Marie's father had to go into hospital on account of his prostate gland.

As Bruce drew up at his temporary abode in Tanner Park Road he was beginning to feel the pressure of life. Apart from the many complicated cases in his work, there were the problems of changing house and the difficulty of not having his family close to him at the time. He would have much preferred a restful evening and so would Marie. However, he had agreed to support the boxing tournament and so they both rushed to unpack and prepare themselves for the evening's entertainment.

As Bruce and Marie drove into the car park at the back of Duckingford Town Hall they noticed that a queue was already building up at the door. The attraction was probably the combination of the celebrities.

As VIPs, Bruce and his wife entered the reception area of the Town Hall, where various officials and councillors were already clustering around the bar. Within seconds, Harry Wilcox, brandishing a half-empty glass of beer, appeared before them. 'Welcome!' he exclaimed with a broad smile. 'Did you have a good journey, Marie? Now let me introduce you to some of our local councillors and activists in the equestrian centre.'

'Everything going smoothly?' enquired Bruce.

'Not exactly,' replied Harry with a concerned look on his face. 'You see we have just discovered that Freddie Barnes has been drinking somewhat heavily during the day and he is hardly in a fit state to enter the ring. However, Harjit Patel appears to be handling the situation and has managed to get a competent stand-in from the Taventry area.'

As Bruce was speaking an anxious Dr Patel, flanked by a brawny, muscular, weather-beaten individual in an ill-fitting suit and who was holding a large cigar in one hand, approached.

'May I introduce our celebrity, Mr Barnes?' Harjit Patel spoke nervously.

Having shaken hands with Bruce and Marie, Freddie Barnes then proceeded to put his arm around Marie's slim figure and ask if he could buy her a drink.

Marie visibly shook with fear. Fortunately, noticing the embarrassment, Harry Wilcox seized the initiative and diverted Freddie's attention to a local admirer who was anxious to obtain his photograph. Both Marie and Bruce were relieved. At that moment Bruce spied Sarah Craig drinking a sherry with two gentlemen admirers. 'Come and meet another of my colleagues,' he said, pulling his wife by the hand.

Sarah had noticed Bruce and his wife from the time that they had entered the building and likewise Marie had not been slow in noticing the odd glance from Sarah in their direction. On being introduced to Bruce's wife, Sarah appeared unusually taciturn and unforthcoming. For a few seconds the two eyed each other cautiously. Marie had heard from Bruce about Sarah's competence in the field of social work and how helpful she had been. She had also heard about Sarah's matrimonial problems and the fact that her husband was now working abroad. Now she had met the person in the flesh she saw how attractive she was, and it was not surprising that Marie felt a little threatened. The meeting between the two, however, was to be short-lived. Hardly had the introduction been completed than Harry Wilcox appeared and announced in a loud voice that the tournament was about to begin and asked the VIPs to make their way to their reserved seats in the gallery.

Bruce and his wife, along with Harry and the others, quickly filed upstairs to their seats. The hall below was full and noisy. Dr Patel could be seen by the ring. He was in charge of First Aid and was accordingly armed with his medical box, prepared for possible injuries. Bruce also picked out Doris Dicker, who had secured a ringside seat and even from the gallery seemed to be in full throttle.

Suddenly a man appeared in the ring clutching the microphone. It was none other than Freddie Barnes. Unsteady on his feet and almost tottering around the ring, he complained to the crowd that the authorities were preventing him, the former world champion, from participating in the tournament because they felt he was unfit. In fact he bawled in a slurred voice, whilst steadying himself against the ropes, that he was ready to take on anyone. The crowd, realising the situation, began to jeer and boo. Quickly two officials jumped into the ring, relieved Freddie of the microphone and guided him out while the official Master of Ceremonies for the evening took the microphone in his hand and began the formalities.

'Ladies and gentlemen,' his voice resonated through the hall, 'tonight we have good news and bad news.'

The crowd groaned.

'The good news is that our referee for the tournament is none other than the famous comedian, your friend and mine, who was born and brought up in this area, the one and only Benny Gayton.'

Pandemonium reigned as the crowd cheered and Benny Gayton stood on a seat at the ringside, his two bodyguards, both wearing evening dress and who normally accompanied him on such occasions, were at his side.

'Thank you,' the MC shouted. 'For your information, Benny has in fact taken a crash course in refereeing and in case of any technical or other problems, we have arranged for another professionally-qualified referee to be at hand to assist if necessary. He is another local lad, Jackie Allsop.'

The crowd again cheered.

The MC continued, 'As you know, this tournament has been specially organised to raise money to set up a riding school for handicapped children in this area. All donations will go to this cause.'

There was a pause.

'And now, ladies and gentlemen, the bad news. As you know, the former World Middleweight Champion, Freddie Barnes, was to give an exhibition tonight but as you may have noted, Freddie is indisposed and unable to compete on account of what could be described as psychosomatic or physiological reasons.'

This gave rise to a number of catcalls and obvious shouts of annoyance.

'He's pissed,' shouted one.

'Bloody drunk,' shouted another. 'Can't hold his liquor.'

The MC attempted to regain control. 'However,' he shouted, 'our local champion, Tommy "Bruiser" Brown, will now be fighting Sugar Ray Pearson from Taventry.'

As cheers rang out, a sack of potatoes was thrown into the ring to be auctioned. This was a period when potatoes were scarce owing to a blight. 'One of our local farmers has very kindly offered a free sack of potatoes to be auctioned for this good cause!' bellowed the MC. 'Have I any offers? One pound, one pound fifty, three pounds…' The sack was soon auctioned for eight pounds, which at that time was nearly twice its normal value.

By this time, to the cheers of the crowd, Benny Gayton had entered the ring. Waving energetically, he strode to the centre and waited whilst the MC introduced him.

'And now,' he shouted, 'your referee *extraordinaire*, the one and only Benny Gayton!'

Benny Gayton took the microphone and, beaming all over and affecting his somewhat effeminate stage voice with its characteristic lisp, he announced, 'Ladies and gentlemen, friends and former school colleagues, good evening!' The crowd loved it and cheered with every sentence.

'Being a comedian is no laughing matter.' He paused while the crowd laughed. 'It is a great honour to be asked to officiate for such an important cause. It's very exciting for me,' again he paused, 'to think of refereeing a match between these handsome male hunks!'

Laughter resounded throughout the hall. The crowd understood well Benny's propensity towards the male gender. Along with his affected lisp, it was an integral part of his routine. 'It's enough to turn you crazy,' Benny went on as the crowd guffawed with laughter. 'Anyway, I've learnt all about refereeing. Did you know that boxers must not touch each other below the belt?' He paused and added, as the laughter subsided, 'What a pity!' He lowered his voice at that last phrase. The crowd continued to shriek with laughter at his double entendres. 'So as a good referee, I am going to make sure that there's no fowling below the belt. Also,' Benny went on, 'you're not allowed to go into clinches for too long. If they do, I'm authorised to go in there with them,' the hilarity continued, 'to break it up of course,' he added. 'So no cuddling, oops I mean, clinching, and no foul play. We don't want anyone to get cocky, do we?'

Guffaws of laughter again rang out.

By this time, the first boxers had entered the ring. Both appeared to be enjoying the banter as much as the audience. 'Tonight I shall be one hundred per cent fair – no favouritism. I intend to give every client, I mean boxer, a fair crack of the whip. Oh!' he gasped as the crowd again sensed an ambiguity in the phrase, 'I didn't mean that kind of whip.' One of the boxers pretended to wince. 'Here, I'd better not say any more,' and Benny handed the microphone back to the MC, who immediately announced the start of the tournament.

As the first participants were being introduced, Harry Wilcox and Bruce Whitford, who were sitting only a few seats apart from each other, exchanged grins of apparent satisfaction with the start of the evening's entertainment.

The supporting bouts of the tournament were entertaining but generally without incident. They involved a number of amateur boxers who demonstrated good craft in the ring but none of whom appeared to possess a knockout punch. The main entertainment in these contests generally came from the gesticulations and capering of the referee, Benny Gayton. On one occasion he temporarily stopped the fight when a boxer appeared to sustain a rather low punch. To the howls of the crowd, Benny asked the fighter if he was all right and appeared to give him a sympathetic stroke on the shorts.

Although the final bout had been rescheduled owing to the indisposition of Freddie Barnes, it nevertheless provided a great deal of interest, since in many ways it was something of a grudge fight. 'Bruiser' Brown and Sugar Ray Pearson had met on two previous occasions, and so far the score was even – they had won one bout each. Both were now eager to prove their superiority over the other. After a rousing build-up by the Master of Ceremonies, the fight got underway and it was not long before blood was drawn. However, this was not one-sided and by round three both boxers had sustained cuts and bruises to the face. It had become quite an exciting match as they traded punch for punch in the middle of the ring. Benny Gayton jumped around frantically, moaning whenever a particularly hard punch went home.

During the interval between each round Benny was seen to consult his advisory referee with great concern. So close was the fight that it was very difficult to pick between the two boxers. By the end of the contest pandemonium reigned. Whose arm was Benny going to raise as the victor? Half the audience seemed to shout for 'Bruiser' and the other half for Sugar Ray. Benny Gayton appeared in despair – he seemed totally confused as he went into deep consultation with the score-takers on either side of the ring as well as with his advisory referee. Eventually a decision was made, and Benny led both boxers to the middle of the ring.

'Ladies and gentlemen,' the MC's voice rang out to a hushed hall, 'after great consultation and consideration, we have finally come to a verdict.' The crowd began to cheer. Benny grinned excessively as he held both boxers' wrists. 'The result,' the MC paused and then again shouted, 'is a draw.'

The crowd cheered as Benny held both boxers' arms in the air and made them turn full circle with short steps like a group of chorus girls. It was a fitting finale to the evening.

Before leaving the Town Hall, Bruce and Marie congratulated Dr Patel and Harry Wilcox on the evening's entertainment. Both appeared pleased with the event although, along with the other members of the committee, they then had the task of counting the money which had been taken at the doors, together with other donations. This had to be bagged and made ready for transfer to the bank.

Bruce and Marie spent the remainder of the weekend exploring Monaston and its environs and generally becoming acquainted with the area. Highlights included a visit to the local museum and a local stately home on the borders of Monaston. Whilst in the borough they also managed to pay another visit to the house in Hatley which they were hoping to purchase. Whilst there, they made an offer for some carpets which the present owners were willing to leave.

When Bruce arrived at the office on Monday, he found Harry Wilcox perusing a copy of an account of the boxing tournament in the local press. 'It was quite a lucrative event all in all,' he informed Bruce. 'We raised almost two thousand pounds. So that will make a useful addition to the funds to date. It shouldn't be too long before we get the equestrian centre off the ground. It's about time too, we have been raising money now for about two years.'

At that point he was interrupted by a secretary who informed him that Mr Thomas, the deputy head of a local comprehensive school, was on the phone.

'Don't tell me,' Harry groaned, 'he's got another extreme case.'

Elwyn Thomas was an articulate Welshman who was very emotional and definite when referring a case. 'Dr Wilcox,' he said in his broad Welsh accent, 'I want you to see a child here. He is literally unteachable. He is twelve years old, comes from Jamaica and cannot read or spell at all. He cannot remember a single word that you teach him. In all my years of teaching, I have never come across such an unteachable child. I can't understand it. I think he needs a special school for children of low intelligence.'

At this point Harry interjected, 'You mean that he cannot read a single word or remember a single word that he is taught?'

'Absolutely,' replied Mr Thomas. 'He is the worst case that I have ever come across.'

'That sounds very serious,' said Harry. Knowing that the best way to deal with Mr Thomas was to nip the situation in the bud, he quickly reflected and continued, 'I tell you what, can you bring him to see me this lunchtime and I will do some preliminary tests to see what we are dealing with? Can you be here with the child at a quarter to one?'

'I shall be there on the dot,' replied Mr Thomas. 'By the way, the boy's name is Winston Dunkley and he is twelve years old.'

'Right,' said Harry, 'I'll see you later,' and he replaced the receiver. For a few moments Harry contemplated, and then he grinned to himself. He had a plan to deal with this situation. Elwyn Thomas had often been on his back complaining about the lack of psychological help his school was receiving so it was time he turned the tables a little.

As Harry reflected, Bruce knocked on his door. 'Come in!' Harry called.

'Harry, can you give me some advice?' asked Bruce. 'I'm on my way to see a Down's Syndrome case in Alfred Street. Am I right in believing that the best placement for the severely educationally impaired is at the Dayland School?'

'Well,' replied Harry, 'there are two points to be made here. First, not all Down's Syndrome cases have severe problems. Some in fact can go to the Blue Lake Special School for ESN pupils and they make fair progress there. These, of course, are the high-grade Down's. But you mentioned Alfred Street. Is the child Indian, as that street is something of a ghetto for Indians?'

'You're absolutely right,' replied Bruce.

'Certain castes or classes of Indians find it difficult to cope with a handicapped child. It is regarded as a slight on their family and I'm afraid to say that when one is assessed as having a handicap, the child is sometimes sent back to India, where rumour has it that he or she is quietly liquidated for money in a back street. That is how some societies deal with their young disabled and at present there is not much we can do about it,' Harry informed him.

Bruce fell silent. He felt confused and to some extent helpless. He thanked Harry for the advice and set off on his domiciliary visit.

Within fifteen minutes he had located the house. Alfred Street was a drab location, consisting of Edwardian terraced houses. He knocked on the door and was invited in by a polite Indian gentleman. The house was sparsely furnished and ill lit. The little girl Bruce had arranged to see was in the back room with her mother. She was poorly clad, wearing what appeared to be a nightdress. No toys were visible. The lack of mental stimulation was only too obvious. Bruce at once noted the characteristic features – high cheek bones, epicanthic folds over the eyes – of

Down's Syndrome. He tried to encourage the child to talk and play with some of the equipment he carried in his testing case. She neither spoke nor showed much understanding of the simplest of instructions, although she was already four years old. Bruce felt her hands, which were soft and rubbery. They indicated hypotonicity or a lack of muscle tone, which was necessary for the purpose of gripping. This was another common feature of Down's Syndrome. It did not take long for Bruce to appreciate that Pritesh, as Mr and Mrs Singh, her parents, called her, had severe learning difficulties and would require a placement at a school for such children. To Bruce, Pritesh appeared to be a low-grade Down's Syndrome child and that meant that she would need special help and a custodial type of environment for a long time.

Bruce picked his words very carefully. Pritesh's parents, who also had three older children, all of whom were doing remarkably well, knew that something was seriously wrong with their youngest child.

'Have you been told by any doctors or nurses that Pritesh has Down's Syndrome?' Bruce asked gently.

The child's parents looked a little perplexed. It was then that Bruce realised that the mother, like so many Indian mothers who had followed their husbands to England, spoke little English.

From then on, Bruce addressed himself to the child's father. 'Your child has a condition which is known as Down's Syndrome,' he continued. 'This means that she will need special educational help. Do you understand?'

Mr Singh nodded. 'How much help will she need before she is normal?' he asked.

'That is hard to answer,' continued Bruce. 'It depends on her progress at the special school. She will be given specialised help in a class where there will only be a small number of pupils. You see, there is a law in England which caters for children with handicaps or learning problems. Any child who has a serious problem, like Pritesh, must be given special help. That is the law.'

'Will she ever be normal?' persisted Mr Singh.

'I cannot give a definite answer to that,' replied Bruce. 'All I can say is that if Pritesh has special help at school she will make progress. It's my job to arrange for Pritesh to be given a place at a school which caters for children who have problems like her and I shall do my best. Are you happy with that?'

Mr Singh did not reply directly. Instead he looked questioningly. Bruce felt that he had done as much as he could in the circumstances and picking up his case, he prepared to leave. His task now was to return to his office and write a report recommending that in view of Pritesh's severe and complex learning difficulties, she should be offered an immediate place at the nursery class in the local special school.

When Bruce arrived back at the office, he noticed a well-dressed man sitting in the waiting room area reading a magazine. It was Elwyn Thomas, the deputy head teacher of a local comprehensive school. As arranged, he had brought his 'unteachable' pupil to be assessed by Harry Wilcox.

Harry was busy in his room administering a short-form intelligence test, and in-between the various tasks which Winston, the boy in question, seemed to be enjoying, Harry took the opportunity of teaching him how to read and spell some rather difficult words by means of memory aids. Over the years Harry, who had a fascination with mnemonics, had amassed a great number of these and his long-term ambition was to produce a booklet entitled 'The Ultimate Book of Mnemonics'. 'Look at this word,' said Harry to Winston. 'It says "moon". See there are two full moons in the middle of it. Can you remember that? Here is another.

It says "eye". It's spelt e-y-e. Imagine a face, and now pretend that the "y" in the middle is the nose and the "e"s on either side are the eyes. So when I show you the word "eye", you will be able to recognise it easily. Next, here is the word "monkey". You can remember that by the "y" on the end which is like a monkey's tail.

'Now,' Harry continued, 'I am going to show you how to remember the spellings of two words. One is easy. It is "said". Remember it like this: "Sally Anne is dancing". So you spell "said" with the first letters of these words.' Harry asked Winston to repeat the words. 'Here is a harder word, "separate". When a "para" jumps he should not separate from his parachute. The two "a"s in "separate" separate the two "e"s.'

By this time Winston appeared to be enjoying the novelty of the approach. During the session, Harry taught and revised twelve different words with Winston. He appreciated that a mastery of reading and spelling involved a great deal more than the teaching of a few tricks. However, Elwyn Thomas had insisted that Winston was unteachable and this was a point which Harry wished to disprove, especially since the intelligence test which he had administered indicated that Winston fell within the normal range.

After about an hour, Harry concluded that he had done all the tests necessary. He had learnt from Winston that the child had only been in the country for about three months, having arrived from a small village in Jamaica where he had hardly attended school at all. Winston came from a rural background where Creole was the common language. Harry had seen it all before. The child was suffering from culture shock, finding himself in a crowded urban community where customs and language were totally different, and where he was expected to attend school every day and do reading and writing, activities which he had seldom done before. Yet, in spite of such disadvantages, Winston demonstrated that he could remember some words.

Harry left Winston in his room whilst he went to talk to Elwyn Thomas. Before leaving the boy, he said, 'I'm just going to go outside for a minute. Whilst I'm outside I want you, Winston, to look at these words and make them your own for the rest of your life. In other words, when I see you in a minute, I want you to get them all right again.' Winston and Harry beamed at each other.

Ever the actor, Harry assumed a worried face as he joined Mr Elwyn Thomas in the waiting area.

'Well, what do you think?' asked Elwyn.

Harry paused. 'I've given Winston a short-form intelligence test and he comes within the normal range in both the verbal and non-verbal areas,' said Harry.

'Yes,' interrupted Mr Thomas, 'but he's unteachable, isn't he?'

'Unteachable?' asked Harry.

'You can't teach him a single word that he will remember,' insisted Mr Thomas. 'He needs to go to a special school, doesn't he?'

'You can't teach him a single word?' questioned Harry.

'That's right. It's all very well for you psychologists with your intelligence tests but we teachers have got to teach reading and spelling.'

Harry gazed through the window in apparent bewilderment. 'You mean to say that if you teach Winston some words, he can't remember them for two minutes?'

'That's right,' replied Elwyn.

Harry took a deep breath and then came out with it. 'You know, Mr Thomas, while I was testing Winston's intelligence I took the opportunity of checking on his memory by teaching him a few words. It didn't take long. Now we've been talking here for some minutes. Shall we go into my room and see if Winston can remember any of the words at all?'

'That I would like to do,' replied Elwyn and they returned to Harry's office, where they found Winston still busy looking at the paper on which Harry had printed some twelve apparently randomly-chosen words.

'How's it going, Winston?' said Harry, giving him a wink. 'I want to see if you can do us a favour. You know those words we were looking at earlier? Yes, these are the ones in front of you. Let's see how many you can remember.' Harry pointed to the word 'dog' and Winston read it with ease. 'Ah good!' remarked Harry. 'Now let's find one that is a little harder.' He pointed to 'moon'. Again Winston read it correctly. 'Well done!' said Harry again. 'And now I'm going to catch you out.' Harry pointed at the word 'separate'. Winston paused and read it with ease.

By this time Elwyn Thomas was staring intensely. He was obviously impressed and by the time Harry had gone through no fewer than twelve words, each of which Winston read with comparative ease, Elwyn appeared almost in a state of shock.

At the conclusion of the exercise, Harry patted Winston on the back and congratulated him and asked him to wait outside for a minute. 'Well,' he said, addressing a rather perplexed Elwyn Thomas, 'I'm sure that I could have taught Winston a lot more if I had had time but you see most of the time was taken up by testing the child's verbal and non-verbal intelligence and also in giving him diagnostic tests to see if his visual and auditory recall is normal. It appears that it is. I'm still not entirely sure what you meant when you said that he was unteachable.'

For a moment, unusually for him, Mr Thomas remained speechless. 'I think I'd better go,' he said. 'I've got a class waiting for me this afternoon.'

'Could you do me a favour?' asked Harry. 'The skills of reading and spelling involve a transfer of knowledge from the short-term memory to the long-term memory. I would like to see if Winston still remembers those words when you get him back to school today and also test him tomorrow, so here's the paper with the words on.'

'Thank you, I certainly will,' replied Elwyn and with that, he hurriedly departed.

Harry smiled to himself and wondered what the outcome of the exercise would be. He would have enjoyed being a fly on the wall when Mr Jones next saw his headmaster or the child's teacher. 'Unteachable,' he muttered to himself as he looked at his watch. 'Ah, just enough time for a bit of lunchtime shopping before the next case.'

Chapter Seven
Lunch at Harry's

It is a common human practice, and perhaps a typically British one, to blithely invite friends and acquaintances to one's home and yet never to arrange a particular date or time on which the invitation could be fulfilled. With some the intention is real or genuine enough but the organisation is lacking, with others there exists little substance from the start. From time to time during his first few months in Monaston, Bruce had been invited by Harry to visit his home in the country. The invitations had been rather non-specific in nature with no definite dates or times arranged and Bruce had not paid much heed to them. However, the latest was different. December had arrived and Marie was to make another weekend trip to the borough. On this occasion Harry insisted that a definite lunch appointment was made for the three of them at his home.

'I may be a failure on many domestic issues,' he proclaimed modestly one morning over coffee, 'but my culinary arts, so my friends tell me, have reached an acceptable standard. So can you and Marie join me in a little pre-Christmas lunch this Saturday?'

'Sounds great to me,' replied Bruce enthusiastically. 'What time do you want us to be at your place, Harry?'

'Shall we say noon or thereabouts?' replied Harry.

Having made a definite arrangement for the meal, Harry began to plan the menu and during the mid-morning break

The boy yelled, 'My mum's a tart.'

he found time to visit the local supermarket for some ingredients. What could they have for a starter? he pondered to himself. Among his favourites were the 'three p's – prawn cocktail, pickled herrings and pea soup. His pea soup would, of course, be home-made, not out of a tin. As Harry scanned the vegetable counter he heard a rumpus behind him. A young boy was repeatedly uttering obscenities.

'Look at those f—king tins! Get out of the bloody way.' His persistent repetition of profanities was far beyond the normal. The boy's mother appeared to continue her shopping, oblivious to the noise. As onlookers stared or turned away in disgust or disbelief, the boy yelled, 'My mum's a tart.'

'I would murder him if that were my child,' commented a lady.

Another, who appeared to know the family, was heard to say, 'They live up the Heathfield Road. The boy goes to Kings Primary School. Thank God he's not in my girl's class! I think he's a bit older than she is.'

Standing nearby, Harry overheard the comments. By this time he had recognised that the child was not in fact having a tantrum but was behaving in a more compulsive way. The longer Harry observed the repetitive and irrational nature of the child's behaviour, the more certain he became of the child's disorder. It could only be Tourette's Syndrome, he concluded to himself. Coprolalia or involuntary and inappropriate swearing was a common characteristic of that condition. The mother was obviously accustomed to the child's bouts of socially unacceptable vocalisations and no doubt realised that her offspring was not in control of himself. Onlookers, however, could easily misconstrue the incident as arising from a lack of parental management. Such is the danger of jumping to conclusions on the evidence of outward behaviour.

His curiosity awakened and ever the psychologist, Harry

by this time had forgotten the main purpose of his visit to the supermarket. Unobtrusively and feigning interest in various vegetables, he moved closer to the boy and his mother. Apart from the persistent swearing, which by this time had become somewhat less vociferous, the child also displayed other mannerisms in keeping with the syndrome. These included periodic deep-knee bends and smelling of the hands, sometimes referred to as tics or involuntary movements.

Harry knew that Tourette's Syndrome, like many disorders, could present itself in moderate or severe form. He also knew that symptoms could be suppressed for periods and are frequently more severe at home than at school or, in the case of adults, in the workplace. They may increase or decrease under strain as well as during relaxation. Like most developmental disorders, the condition should be identified as early as possible and appropriate help given. Treatment was a multi-disciplinary affair and embraced both psychosocial measures and pharmacological intervention. Harry was aware that, ideally, the patient should be referred to a consultant or centre specialising in the disorder. He knew of one in the London area.

Having completed his purchases, Harry returned promptly to the office. His aim was to contact Nancy Holland, the head teacher of Kings Primary School, during the lunch hour. In particular, his curiosity had been aroused by the fact that a child with such a severe disorder had not already been referred to the Psychological Service. On arriving in the typing pool of the SPS, Harry, preoccupied with his thoughts, hardly acknowledged Bruce Whitford and Delia Berry as he brushed past them. His two colleagues were in fact busy discussing plans for a two-pronged approach to the case of a seven-year-old boy from Dorley Village on the outskirts of Monaston, who had recently been referred to them for stealing and other antisocial activities. Arrangements had been made for Bruce to visit the child's school to discuss the case with the teachers and possibly carry out some psychological tests. Meanwhile Delia would visit the child's home, take a full history of the child and discuss the problem with his mother. Bruce himself would then go on to the home, at which time the father should have returned from work and a full family discussion could take place. Hopefully, some constructive suggestions might be offered. Such were the plans being carefully formulated in the office at that moment. Whether they would be as smoothly implemented remained to be seen.

'How are you, Nancy?' Harry could be heard in his office as he greeted Miss Holland over the phone. She was the long-suffering head teacher of Kings Primary School who had risen from the post of assistant teacher through to deputy head, and was now head of the same school, never transferring to another establishment throughout her long teaching career. She boasted that one day she would be teaching the grandchildren of those she had once taught as a young teacher.

'I'm fine,' replied Nancy, 'and you?'

'I'll come to the point, Nancy,' replied Harry. 'I was downtown in a supermarket this lunchtime and, along with other shoppers, saw a child swearing persistently at the top of his voice. It was no ordinary tantrum or loss of temper. It just persisted and when I got closer he also showed a number of tics – you know, uncontrollable movements. Every so often he also bent his legs or smelt his hands.'

'Don't tell me,' interrupted Nancy, 'you're talking about our Dale.'

'Dale?' asked Harry.

'Yes, little Dale Bentley,' continued Nancy. 'He was out with his mother at lunchtime because the school dinner ladies can no longer handle him. They talk about his filthy language and odd behaviour and his mother says that it's the same at home. Strangely enough, he is not a great problem in the classroom – does his work and the teachers seldom complain of him, although he does grunt at times and occasionally yelps like a dog – but we can live with it.'

'It's beginning to fall into place,' said Harry. 'It's my feeling that the boy is suffering from Tourette's Syndrome. Have you ever heard of this complaint?'

'No,' replied Nancy.

'Well, it's a kind of obsessional compulsive disorder and the symptoms are exactly as you have described and I have seen. The boy probably cannot help these tics or other odd habits. He can partially control them in school but once outside, the lid comes off. Have you ever heard of the term "coprolalia", Nancy?'

'You're getting very technical,' replied Nancy.

'Well,' continued Harry slowing his speech a little, 'it's just a fancy psychological term referring to an uncontrollable urge to utter obscenities or swear. Believe it or not, these individuals cannot stop themselves. There's no reason for it. It's like a sneeze – you know it's coming but you cannot stop it. So far you seem to have handled Dale very well, but unfortunately Tourette's is a serious disorder and as the child gets older it can cause all kinds of relationship problems; some of these children become social lepers.

'Another point about the disorder is that it sometimes runs in families. Siblings, parents or other relations may also show odd behaviour.'

At this point Nancy interrupted, 'Harry, you're not going to believe this but I taught Dale's father, Richard. He was rather odd as a child. He's now a postman. He frequents The Griffin Inn, the local pub up here, and is well known for his odd habit of twitching his neck as he props up the bar. In fact his nickname is "Rich the Twitch".'

'Interesting,' replied Harry, continuing, 'I understand

that there are some medicines available now which can help to control the disorder. I know of a centre in London which specialises in the condition. We would need to contact the child's family doctor, of course, and also the paediatrician. Initially I would like to arrange a home visit by Delia Berry. Is that all right with you?'

'Of course,' replied Nancy, 'anything to help the child. I will try to see his mother this afternoon to prepare the way.'

'Many thanks, Nancy,' replied Harry and he hurriedly put the phone down and rushed to the door, hoping to catch Delia Berry. He was, however, too late.

'Mrs Berry went a few minutes ago,' Tina, the typist, informed him. 'She went off at the same time as Mr Whitford. I believe they've gone out to Dorley Village.'

By this time both Bruce and Delia were well on their way to their respective appointments, one to Dorley Primary School and the other to a home in a road adjacent to the school. Like many of the villages in the area, Dorley had grown up around a local coal mine. The church and its adjoining primary school were the central features of the village. The coal mine itself was run down and as a result unemployment and poverty were common in the area, and single parent families were on the increase.

Ena Large was the head teacher of Dorley Primary. She was a familiar figure in the village and her name to some extent befitted her morphology. Ena was a corpulent middle-aged lady with a jovial smile and a friendly disposition. Afternoon school had begun and she greeted Bruce as he entered the main entrance of the building.

'What are your plans?' Ena enquired. 'Do you want to see the child right away or shall we discuss the case first?'

'I find that it can be useful if I first see the child "blind", as it were,' replied Bruce. 'I could carry out some tests and then, hopefully, may be able to add something to our discussion afterwards, if you're happy with that, Mrs

Large?'

Ena readily agreed to the plan of action and went off to fetch Jimmy Barratt, the seven-year-old who was at the centre of the investigation, while Bruce set up his testing material in a corner of the school library. Within minutes, Ena reappeared accompanied by a confident little boy with a freckled face and deep, brown eyes. 'You have been specially chosen today to do some tests for this gentleman,' she confided to her small companion, 'so do your best, Jimmy,' and Ena disappeared.

Meanwhile, not far away in one of the terraced cottages built for miners at the turn of the century, Delia Berry was being welcomed into the child's home by Mrs Barratt, a shapely peroxide blonde in her mid-twenties. She wore a red jumper and black miniskirt of pelmet proportions. Delia was ushered into the living room where an elderly man was reading a newspaper in an armchair on one side of a blazing fire. Standing almost in front of the fire was a metal frame covered in nappies. Mrs Barratt picked up the frame and put it to one side. 'This is Granddad's zimmer,' she said. 'We got it free from the hospital. It's very good for drying the twins' nappies on!'

Delia, who herself often supported applications for various appliances, looked a little perturbed, and then replied, 'Yes. I understand that you have twins.'

'They're over at my mother's at the moment,' Mrs Barratt continued. 'She offered to look after them whilst I spoke to you. It's so much quieter without the twins. You know, they have completely taken over our lives.'

'Twins are known to be double trouble,' said Delia.

'Oh, they are no trouble,' went on Mrs Barratt. 'They're wonderful!'

At this point the elderly gentleman sitting in the armchair interjected with a smile, 'They are wonderful. They are already beginning to walk. We can't remember what life was like before them.'

'I always wanted a girl,' said Mrs Barratt, 'and now we have two beautiful ones.' For the next few minutes she proceeded to extol the wonders of her babies until Delia, as tactfully as possible, indicated that the real point of her visit was to discuss the problems which Mrs Barratt's eldest child, Jimmy, had been manifesting recently, in particular his habit of stealing.

'I can't understand him,' remarked Mrs Barratt. 'He's been stealing pencils from his school and he doesn't need them because his daddy brings home plenty from the office.' Mr Barratt was a surface worker in the office at Dorley Mine. 'Jimmy seems to be deliberately causing trouble and he knows that I have my work cut out with Josie and Jasmin, the twins.'

'Perhaps he's trying to say something,' suggested Delia.

Mother and grandfather paused and looked at her questioningly. Delia chose her words carefully, 'Since you've had the twins, you say yourself life has changed. A great deal of your attention has been given to the twins. You also mentioned that you preferred girls to boys. Do you think it is possible that since the twins were born, Jimmy has felt a little neglected or even pushed out?'

Mrs Barratt was obviously upset with what she was listening to. The truth often hurts. She looked at the children's grandfather who had been pondering on the suggestions. He looked up and remarked, 'In fact in the last few weeks I have felt the same. Perhaps we're all to blame. Jimmy was once the centre of our life and now it's the twins. Perhaps he feels shut out and we haven't bothered to notice it. But Denise, there is something else that you were going to tell Mrs Berry. Don't you think it's time?'

'Oh, yes,' Denise Barratt agreed, suddenly springing to life. 'This is terrible,' she said. 'There is a lady next door who only moved in a few weeks ago. Each day a mother whom I've seen down the shops, I don't know her name, brings a toddler, he can't be more than two, in a pushchair and leaves him with her.'

'Your neighbour is probably being paid as a child-minder,' remarked Delia.

'Yes, fair enough,' continued Mrs Barratt. 'But listen to this. As soon as the mother has gone, the woman puts the little child into the lavatory in the back yard, closes the door and leaves him there. Sometimes she goes out for hours on end and leaves the poor little mite in the dark there.'

'How long has this been going on?' Delia asked in amazement.

'It could be at least two weeks,' replied Denise Barratt and added, 'I just happened to notice this a few days ago. It's happened each day since and I've been waiting for you to come to tell you. Is it illegal?'

'It certainly is,' Delia remarked with incredulity. 'I think the little boy is in there right now and the woman has gone off probably to play bingo or something in Monaston.' Denise added, 'Would you like to come upstairs and see where she leaves him?'

Delia followed Denise Barratt up the stairs to the landing where the back yard of the next house could be seen through a small window. 'You can see the lavatory next to the coal shed,' Denise indicated and added, 'I'm sure the little mite is in there now.'

'May I use your phone?' asked Delia as they returned downstairs.

'Certainly. It's in the back room,' replied Denise, leading the way.

During the next ten minutes Delia made a series of frantic calls. There was a code of practice concerning cruelty to children which local authority officers were expected to follow. In the first place, the Social Services department should be informed. Delia, who was employed by the Education department and whose relationship with Social Services was, to say the least, problematic, decided first to ring her friend, Roger Judson, the police liaison officer, and then the NSPCC. After that she would ring Harry Wilcox and suggest that he rang the Social Services. 'Your neighbour deserves what's coming to her,' she muttered to Mrs Barratt between calls.

Meanwhile down the road in Dorley Primary, Bruce Whitford was coming to the end of his interview with Jimmy Barratt. Psychometric tests had not disclosed anything of significance. Jimmy appeared to be a child of normal intelligence who was working approximately to his age and ability level in the basic subjects of reading, spelling and arithmetic. However, some interesting points had arisen when Bruce had invited Jimmy to participate in a family relationship test. The test material consisted of a number of cardboard figures, each of which could be used to represent a member of a child's family. The child was asked a series of questions concerning members of the family. Examples of such questions were: Who would you like to go on holiday with? Who is your favourite friend in the family? Who annoys you the most? The child would answer by selecting the particular cardboard figures which represented the characters chosen and then place them in a particular box.

As the activity proceeded, Bruce soon realised that Jimmy's affections were seldom directed towards his twin sisters. In fact, it was not difficult to deduce that he had many negative thoughts about his younger siblings, and that his behavioural difficulties could well be linked to this. Was Jimmy's antisocial behaviour really a cry for help? Since the advent of the twins, had he felt neglected or rejected?

After the interview with Jimmy, it was playtime and Bruce was able to have a chat with both the child's teacher and the head teacher, Mrs Large, in the latter's office.

Bruce's suggestion that Jimmy's problems arose out of attention-seeking factors or feelings of isolation in his own home were soon taken on board. Both teachers agreed that the stealing incidents had only occurred since the birth of the twins and in many ways his recent misdemeanours were uncharacteristic. Ena Large also observed that she had rarely seen Mrs Barratt during the past year whereas at one time she had been a regular visitor to the school.

'The home visit should be an interesting one,' Bruce remarked, and added as he prepared to leave, 'No doubt by now Delia Berry has made her own diagnosis. I wonder if it tallies with ours?'

Within minutes Bruce had arrived at the Barratts' home. He parked his car several houses away since a number of vehicles had already taken the available spaces. In fact, the place seemed to be buzzing with activity. Bruce was puzzled. Not only was Roger Judson and another police officer standing outside the Barratts' home but Jim Dyer, the local NSPCC officer, was alighting from his car and joining them.

'Why is it so busy?' enquired Bruce as he joined the others at the door of the Barratts' home.

'I think Delia will be able to enlighten you,' replied Roger Judson with a concerned look on his face as the door opened and both Mrs Barratt and Delia Berry appeared. The group were ushered into the house and Bruce soon learnt the purpose of the gathering. It was, in fact, nothing to do with the Barratt family but concerned their next door neighbours.

'So we understand that there is a little child locked in the lavatory next door. This has been going on for some time and the childminder disappears for hours on end,' said Roger Judson.

'I'm afraid so,' replied Denise Barratt. 'But I only discovered it for sure a few days ago.'

'And as far as you know he is in there now?' Roger queried.

'Yes,' replied Denise.'

'Right,' said Roger. 'I've got a search warrant. We will now have to take action. I suggest that in the first place we divert attention away from this house. Remember, you have got to live with this neighbour so the less she feels you are involved,' Roger addressed Mrs Barratt, 'the better. First I'm going to ask my colleague here to climb over the back wall and then unlock the back door and let Mrs Berry and Jim Dyer into the yard. It will probably be less upsetting for the little boy if a lady opens the lavatory door first and tries to lessen the shock for him. Would you be willing to do that, Delia?' Mrs Berry nodded in agreement. 'The rest of you can watch operations from the upstairs window and if necessary you could always act as further witnesses, but I doubt whether it will come to that.'

Within minutes Roger Judson's colleague had scaled the back wall of the neighbour's house and had let Delia and Jim Dyer into the yard. Cautiously Delia approached the door of the outside toilet and lifted the latch, which was too high for any toddler to reach. Slowly she opened the door and peered inside. Huddled in the shadows in the corner beside the pedestal was a tiny boy. His eyes blinked as the light penetrated the gloom. He remained silent and motionless. A dummy lay on the floor in front of him. Delia picked up the dummy and held out her hands to the little toddler. Failing to elicit a response, she advanced and, taking the child by the hand, lifted him up and with some soothing words of encouragement brought him into the fresh air. The little mite, with a somewhat stiff and unsteady gait, followed her compliantly as all around gazed in wonder and sympathy.

'What are you called? What is your name?' Delia asked gently. The child remained speechless. Whether he could

Huddled in the shadows in the corner beside the pedestal was the figure of a tiny boy.

speak at all was questionable. No one could guess what was going on in the tormented privacy of that little mind. Despite having normal intellectual potential, children who lack verbal stimulation, or indeed any kind of stimulation during the early years, can fail to develop speech or at best, would suffer from speech delay which could blight their development for the rest of their life. Recent research, as Bruce was well aware, also indicated that the persistent use of a dummy could inhibit language growth. The sad little figure who had just emerged from his dark prison did not appear to have enjoyed many of life's privileges.

It had been agreed that the child should be taken immediately to the police station, accompanied by Jim Dyer, the NSPCC officer, and Delia Berry. Roger Judson's colleague would drive them there and then come back. Roger himself would wait for the return of the lady who was responsible for the care of the child. He would wait in the front room of the Barratts.

Having collected his thoughts after the traumatic events of the last half hour, Bruce suggested to Mrs Barratt that they sit down and have a chat about the original reason for his visit, which concerned the recent behavioural problems of her son, Jimmy. Accordingly, they both retired to the living room whilst Roger Judson, now armed with a mug of coffee, kept a close eye on the road outside from the front room.

'Mrs Berry believes that Jimmy's behaviour may be our fault. Since we have had the twins they have dominated our life and maybe little Jimmy feels pushed out,' said Denise Barratt, lowering her head and staring at the floor in a forlorn manner.

'Don't reproach yourself,' said Bruce, who as a father was well-aware of the difficulties of parenting. 'None of us is perfect and we are all learning. When you buy a washing machine or a camera, it usually comes with a set of instructions but it is not like that with children, so we normally learn by experience. When children misbehave we give them attention so if they feel that they need attention, they soon learn that they can get it by being naughty. It may be that that is exactly what Jimmy has been doing.'

'So what's the answer?' asked Denise.

'Well,' said Bruce, 'first you need to concentrate on the positive points. Praise him for what he's good at. For instance, you could say that the man who came to see him today was pleased with his schoolwork, and that the teachers were pleased as well. Ignore as far as possible any naughtiness. If he tries to get your attention by misbehaving make sure that it doesn't work. On the other hand, make sure that you also give him some of your time. Children need time, not material things. I know that you are a very busy woman, Mrs Barratt,' Bruce continued, 'but it could make all the difference if you could find some time during the day to do things on your own with Jimmy, in other words, give him some attention. There is no better way of getting to know a child than to play with him.'

At that moment, Bruce and Denise Barratt heard movements from the front room. Roger Judson had been quietly sipping coffee near the front window when he suddenly caught sight of a middle-aged lady in a blue anorak and red trousers carrying a shopping bag, who was standing on the steps of the house next door.

'Come and see,' said Roger, popping his head round the door of the living room. Immediately Denise Barratt leapt to her feet and went into the front room.

'That's her,' she said, indicating the lady on the steps.

'Leave it to me,' replied Roger. Within seconds he had quietly vacated the house and as if appearing from nowhere, was standing behind the next door neighbour, who was fiddling with her keys in the lock of the door.

'Excuse me, Madam,' remarked Roger. 'Could I possibly

have a few words with you?'

Turning round, the woman looked Roger up and down suspiciously and replied, 'Why?'

'I'm a police officer,' continued Roger 'and I understand that you are being paid to look after a little boy.'

'How do I know that you are a police officer? You haven't got a uniform,' said the woman.

'I have identification here,' replied Roger 'and that is my car waiting for me over there.' He pointed to the police car driven by his colleague who had now returned from the station and parked deliberately about twenty yards from the house.

'So what is the problem?' asked the woman.

'We understand that you have been regularly locking a little child in the lavatory in your back yard and leaving him alone for hours on end.'

'That's lies,' answered the woman. 'I've only ever done it once and that's today because it was an emergency.'

'I'm asking you, Madam,' interrupted Roger, 'to accompany me to the police station where we can discuss the matter in detail.'

'What about the child?' the woman asked.

'The child is at the police station,' replied Roger.

'Oh,' she replied. 'Then you leave me no option.'

Not particularly visible since they were standing back from the window, Bruce and Denise Barratt were able to observe Roger Judson's encounter with the neighbour. They listened intently but could hardly decipher the content of the conversation. Eventually they watched the two figures walk down the road and get into the police car, which immediately drove off.

'So what will happen to her?' enquired Denise.

Bruce reflected for a few moments. 'I should imagine that she will give her version of the story down at the station. The police will check her record, if she has one, and will confirm the identity of the child. They will then contact the child's parents, inform them of the incident and invite them to the police station. Social Services and the Health department will be alerted. An inquiry will be made into the background of the child, who may well be referred to us later for a full psychological assessment.'

'And what about that woman? What will happen to her?' asked Denise.

'Depends what they find out,' replied Bruce. 'She will probably be given a rap over the knuckles and get away with it. Of course if Social Services find other conditions of neglect in the child's background, then he may be placed in care. The thing which bothers me about this business is how much damage has been done to that child's mind and body already by the way he has been treated.'

Bruce decided that it was time to leave. He bade farewell to Mrs Barratt, promised to check on her son's progress in the near future and left the house.

The weekend soon arrived. Bruce and Marie had planned to spend it exploring Monaston and the surrounding countryside. The situation with regard to their moving home was still going through a difficult phase. In particular the purchase chain concerning their own property had experienced a hiccup and both Bruce and Marie were loath to take out a bridging loan in order to ensure the purchase of the Monaston house which they hoped to buy. Both realised that a bridging loan could be very expensive, since there was no guarantee as to how long it might continue. They had, therefore, decided to adopt a philosophical approach and put domestic issues in the background in order to enjoy the weekend for what it was worth.

Saturday morning arrived and Bruce and Marie soon found themselves driving up to the Earl of Beersford's estate. Harry had given precise directions. They would enter the estate on the south side, passing through large wrought-iron gates which were normally open with a lodge on the left. After proceeding up the main drive for about two hundred yards, they would bear right on to a small country road, flanked by open ground on one side and woods on the other. After about three quarters of a mile, they would come to a group of cottages dotted alongside the road. Harry's residence was the second cottage on the right.

Bruce and Marie were in a carefree mood as they passed through the main entrance of the estate. As they proceeded up the drive, the Earl of Beersford's stately and imposing home loomed in the distance. 'I trust that's not Harry's place,' remarked Marie with a chuckle.'

'He's well heeled,' replied Bruce, 'but I don't think Harry is that rich.' Within minutes, they had branched off on the road to the right and were in sight of the cottages.

'What a charming rural setting!' said Marie as they came to a halt near the gate of the second cottage.

Bruce made no comment. Instead he was staring intently at a thick-set little man who was bent over what appeared to be a small compost heap at the end of the cottage garden. 'That doesn't look like Harry,' he remarked. 'Perhaps he has a gardener.'

The couple got out of their car, opened the cottage gate and proceeded up the path to the door. As they passed the crouched figure, Bruce politely said, 'Good afternoon.'

As the figure turned and offered a full frontal view, Bruce immediately recognised the characteristic high cheek bones, rounded head and epicanthic folds around the eyes of a young man with Down's Syndrome. 'Hello,' he replied with a smile. 'Dr Wilcox is cooking.'

'You're right, Lenny,' came a voice from the porch as Harry suddenly appeared at the door. 'I see you have met my efficient gardener, Lenny,' continued Harry as he welcomed Bruce and Marie into the cottage.

'So Lenny works for you?' enquired Bruce. 'He certainly does,' replied Harry. 'He's a good gardener – very routine as you might expect, a bit inflexible but keeps the place tidy and is very good at making compost. A good compost heap consists of muck and magic. I'll give you the recipe, Bruce, if you're ever interested. Lenny keeps the garden in the same way as I manage my shares on the stock exchange; my motto is 'cut out the weeds and cultivate the flowers'. Harry continued, 'I've known Lenny since he was born. As a matter of fact, when we first learnt that Lenny had Down's Syndrome I was at hand to give his mother a bit of counselling. He still lives with his mother a few cottages along. No one knows much about the father. Some say Lenny could have blood relations in high places.' Harry spoke in a lowered tone with his tongue in his cheek. 'Anyway, enough of rumours! Lenny was trained by the head gardener up at the estate and I'm lucky to have him working for me.'

At that moment a beautiful pedigree cat with long, sleek, white hair flecked with cream and blue walked gracefully into the hall. 'This is Duchess, my Himalayan colourpoint,' said Harry beaming proudly, adding, 'Although I love my hounds, a dog is basically a prize, whereas a cat is poetry.'

'Isn't she gorgeous!' remarked Marie.

'She certainly is,' added Bruce as he bent down to stroke her. Unimpressed, Duchess turned and walked disdainfully away, leaving Bruce at a full knee-bend stroking the air.

'Don't be offended,' said Harry. 'She's a snob like her owner – a real "aristocat". At the moment she's even giving me the cold shoulder since I took her to the vet's earlier in the week. It took three of us to get a worming tablet down her.

'Now, Marie, Bruce,' Harry continued, 'how about an aperitif, a sherry or maybe something stronger?'

'A sherry is fine for me,' replied Marie.

'And the same for me,' added Bruce.

'Sweet? Dry? Medium?' queried Harry.

'We're both middle of the road,' said Bruce. 'Medium would be excellent.'

Whilst Harry was busy pouring drinks from his cabinet, Marie's eye had been caught by some of the Victorian paintings hanging in his lounge.

'What beautiful pictures!' she commented.

'They're my pride and joy,' said Harry, pausing and looking up from the drinks cabinet. 'What do you think of the one over the mantelpiece?'

'Striking, to say the least,' remarked Bruce.

'It's a masterpiece,' interjected Harry, 'mid-Victorian, painted, signed and dated by Charles Edward Johnson. It's worth a bit, that one, and is well insured. Johnson has one of his works hanging in the Tate.'

Armed with their drinks, Marie and Bruce soon found themselves on a conducted tour of the cottage. Not only were they given detailed accounts of each painting, every one an original, but they were also shown some of Harry's antique treasures, which included a grandfather clock dating from the eighteenth century, a highly-polished wainscot chair and a bookcase from the Regency period. Some smaller items were also on show, including a solid silver goblet and a small, delicately-painted Japanese vase.

'An exquisite piece of virtuosity, don't you think?' said Harry as he proudly held the ornament aloft for all to see.

'Yes,' commented Bruce. 'Not exactly bric-a-brac!'

'And now let's turn our minds to more mundane things,' said Harry with a flourish. 'In short, sustenance, nutrition or, if you wish, just plain food.'

'Is that what we're going to get, Harry – just plain food?' asked Bruce, tongue in cheek.

Marie retained a polite silence.

'Well, perhaps not too plain,' replied Harry, adding, 'and, on the other hand, not too exotic. I will leave you to judge the proof of the pudding,' he said with a smile. 'You have a choice of starter – either home-made pea soup or pickled herrings.'

'We're spoilt for choice – I like both,' replied Bruce.

'I think I'll go for pea soup,' said Marie.

'To retain variety, I'll have the pickled herring if that's okay with you,' added Bruce.

'They're both okay with me,' replied Harry. 'Now come this way.'

The dining room was in the back of the house. Bruce and Marie had hardly sat down and tucked their napkins into place when Harry reappeared from the kitchen with the starters all prepared. Marie had her steaming pea soup and Bruce his pickled herrings.

'That's what I call service,' remarked Bruce as he delicately savoured his first taste. 'Have you always cooked for yourself, Harry?'

'Well, not always,' replied Harry. 'In fact, I once employed a cook who, to quote Saki, was good, as good cooks go – and as good cooks go, she went! I must say that during the relatively short time she was with me, I learnt quite a lot about cuisine.'

For the next two hours the conversation flowed easily. A variety of subjects was covered, from the inadequacies of the local authorities and governments to the pros and cons of fox-hunting. Being aware of Harry's views about the latter subject, both Bruce and Marie deliberately maintained a diplomatic reticence, as to some extent did Harry. 'Don't misunderstand me,' he insisted. 'I am well aware of the arguments against hunting and I must confess that, along with many of my colleagues, I am often secretly glad when Old Renard gets away. But have you ever seen a whole coop of chickens savaged by a couple of foxes – all their legs bitten off in sheer bloodthirstiness, and not just to eat? I've actually seen that.' Harry appeared deliberately to prolong the interval between courses and this certainly did not bother either Bruce or Marie, who were enjoying the unusual hospitality. 'As the French say,' Harry remarked, 'eating is the art of waiting.'

By the time the cheese course had appeared, Marie and Bruce were feeling well satisfied, although they made room for a little of their favourite cheeses before coffee. 'I love Double Gloucester,' remarked Marie, cutting off a moderate portion of the same.

'And as for me, I always go for the strong stuff, Stilton,' added Bruce, as he cut a sizeable portion.

'Oh, yes, why not?' said Harry who, noting Bruce's choice, couldn't resist the cue to impart some important information. 'We deprecate the French,' he said, 'for eating frogs, the Welsh for eating seaweed and the Chinese for consuming snakes and locusts but did you know that Stilton cheese is made from the secretion of live animals which is left to rot and go mouldy?'

'Is that so?' said Bruce, placing a piece of cheese on his plate and looking somewhat uncomfortable.

'Don't let it bother you, Bruce,' said Harry, tongue in cheek. 'Stilton is also my favourite.'

As with most convivial occasions, time seemed to pass quickly and it wasn't long before Bruce and Marie found themselves at the cottage gate, thanking Bruce for his excellent hospitality. Although dusk was approaching, there appeared to be plenty of life in the vicinity. A rider, exercising his horse, cantered by within fifty yards of them. Harry gave a wave and the rider held up his crop to acknowledge it.

'That's Austin Rathbone,' remarked Harry, adding with a smile, 'an impressive name but no pedigree.'

Just then another of Harry's neighbours passed, carrying

a brace of rabbits in one hand and a sack in the other.

'Good evening, Ted,' called Harry.

'Good evening, Sir,' replied the man dutifully touching his forelock.

Harry waited for the man to get out of earshot before commenting with a twinkle in his eye, 'That's Ted Fenn, one of our gamekeepers. Lives over in Badger's Cottage,' he added, gesticulating to the right. 'He knows his place as you can see from the salutation. What do you think he has in the sack?'

'Haven't a clue,' replied Bruce.

'A ferret,' answered Harry. 'Ted is off ferreting rabbits. In fact I sometimes buy the odd one from him myself. Could be illegal, I'm not sure. We country folk don't ask questions. We live and let live.'

At that moment the attention of all three was drawn to what appeared to be the crack of a rifle off to the right. 'A bit late for shooting pigeons,' remarked Harry and then pointing in the same direction, he indicated a figure tearing across the meadow. 'That's Ted Fenn's boy, Jake. He's moving like a bat out of Hell! He's probably put a pellet through a window or something. Beware, Bruce. That boy is a problem, another teenager with hormones and misdirected energy. He's been suspended twice from school already – a nasty piece of work, always in trouble and he's now on your patch.'

'Thanks,' replied Bruce in a tone of resignation and with that, both he and Marie climbed into their car, waved goodbye and drove back the way they had come.

As they neared the gates of the estate they heard the siren of an ambulance as well as that of a police car. They had hardly passed through the gates when to their amazement an ambulance, pursued closely by a police car, turned in the way they had come out. 'Action on the estate,' commented Bruce.

'Yes,' said Marie. 'You never know. It could be connected to that boy we saw running away after the gun shot.'

'Could be?' said Bruce ponderingly.

'Well, I think we failed in one thing,' remarked Marie.

'What?' asked Bruce. 'We were hoping to learn a little more about Harry's background,' said Marie, 'but he is still something of a mystery.'

Bruce pondered for a few minutes and then muttered, 'Yes, I suppose you're right.'

Monday morning soon arrived. Although Bruce was early in the office, Harry had preceded him and was already going through the post at his own desk. 'Can you spare a moment, Bruce?' called Harry as Bruce passed the door of his office, which had been left open.

'Certainly,' replied Bruce. 'Is it serious?'

Harry paused. 'You could say serious,' he replied slowly and after further reflection, added, 'Very serious.'

Bruce looked concerned and Harry, enjoying keeping his colleague on tenterhooks, deliberately took his time.

'Well,' he said eventually, 'you remember last Saturday as we were saying goodbye outside the cottage?'

'Yes,' replied Bruce.

'Well,' continued Harry, 'do you remember we heard a rifle shot and that was followed by a youth tearing across the meadow?'

'I remember,' said Bruce in anticipation.

'Well,' Harry went on, still in an unhurried manner and making the most of the occasion, 'you remember just before that incident a gamekeeper passed with a brace of rabbits and a sack.'

'I remember,' replied Bruce. 'He had a ferret in the sack.'

'Exactly,' said Harry 'and that was Ted Fenn. I have known the family for years. His teenage son, Jake, whom I warned you about, was the youth running across the meadow, and the bang we heard came from an air gun. It now appears that the boy shot his mother.'

'Shot his mother!' gasped Bruce. 'Is she dead?'

'Fortunately not,' replied Harry. 'But she was injured enough to have to be taken to hospital.

'After you left on Saturday things became quite busy. In fact we had the police here and an ambulance. Poor Beryl Fenn was taken away on a stretcher. But that's not the end of the matter. Apparently it wasn't a case of an argument in which the rifle went off. It seems that Jake had been misbehaving again and was grounded by his parents for the weekend. The boy called for his mother. She came out of the kitchen to see him staring down the barrel of his father's air gun and he shot at her in cold blood. He then absconded and was picked up by the police, sitting on his grandmother's grave in the cemetery in a foetal position. Jake is now under lock and key in a detention centre and his father is so distraught that he claims that he never wants to set eyes on the boy again. So there you are, Bruce,' concluded Harry. 'It's quite a serious family situation. No doubt you will be asked to carry out a full psychological assessment in the not too distant future. Rather you than me!'

Bruce stood perplexed for a moment and then gathering his thoughts, said, 'I assume there will be a cooling-off period?'

'Oh, yes,' replied Harry. 'And when the administration decide that something must be done with the boy, they will no doubt approach you for recommendations and perhaps it may be useful to first ask Delia Berry to report on the home situation before carrying out your own assessment. Anyway, that could be weeks off. Meanwhile I must away to collect my first case of the day, another backward reader, would you believe?' and with that, Harry left his room and went to the waiting area to collect a little eight-year-old boy with dark curls and rosy cheeks, who had been patiently waiting with his mother.

Bruce was about to enter his own office when Jesse Fry, the education welfare officer with whom he had gone on a weekend course a month or so before and who at the time was busy talking to Irene Cathcart, the senior secretary, called his name. 'Bruce,' he said, 'can you spare a moment?'

'Come in and sit yourself down,' replied Bruce. 'I haven't seen you for some time. How are you?'

'Well,' replied Jesse, relaxing on a chair in Bruce's office, 'you recall that some weeks ago you helped us make contact with our long-lost son, Tommy?'

'I believe I suggested that you wrote to the Sally Army about him,' replied Bruce.

'Exactly,' Jesse went on, 'and we did and they very kindly forwarded a letter from us to him. Well,' he continued, 'that was the last we heard of the matter until this weekend when a very strange thing happened.'

'Go on,' said Bruce, in eager anticipation.

'You're going to find this very hard to believe, Bruce,' said Jesse as he again gathered his breath and continued. 'Did I tell you that our eldest daughter, Fiona, is studying to be a doctor and she is in her last year of university?'

'Yes, you did,' replied Bruce, still listening intently. 'Well,' said Jesse again, 'at the moment she is working as a medical student in the casualty department at the General Hospital down south in Portsmouth. Last Saturday night a patient who had been involved in a street brawl was brought in by the police to be stitched up. The secretary who checks the patients in happened to mention to my daughter that someone with her surname had been admitted. When she checked on the Christian name, she was amazed – it was Tommy. She then went to look for herself and sure enough, before she even got to the treatment room, she could hear Tommy arguing with the nurses.

'She plucked up courage and looked behind the screen to be greeted by her brother, "Fiona, what the hell are you doing here?"

"Exactly what I was going to say to you," replied Fiona. It appears that Tommy had got in a fight with some sailors outside a pub in Pompey and had ended up with a number of cuts and a fractured arm.'

'What a coincidence!' gasped Bruce.

'It's incredible, isn't it?' said Jesse, adding, 'To think of all the hospitals Tommy could have ended up in, it was the one where his sister was working. Well, I shall keep you posted and let you know if he rings. Fiona has made him promise to do so and he has agreed. I must go now. I've got some truants to chase up,' and he left Bruce's room.

Bruce sat on his chair to gather breath. He pondered over the news he could tell Marie on the phone that night. First there was the affair concerning the gamekeeper's son and now the unbelievable coincidence concerning the missing Tommy Fry. It would be good if Tommy did make contact with his parents, he thought to himself as he began to go through the pile of documents from his in-tray. He had hardly begun to read the first letter when he heard a knock on his door.

'Come in,' Bruce called. It was Delia Berry, full of life as usual. Bruce could tell by her manner that she had something of interest to say and it was apparently confidential, judging from the way she carefully closed the door.

'So what do you think?' Delia asked.

'What do I think about what?' replied Bruce, thinking that Delia was about to inform him about the shooting incident involving the gamekeeper's son and, when she had finished giving her account, he would surprise her by saying that he had actually been nearby at the time. However, both were at cross purposes.

'You know,' Delia continued and pointed to her eye.

'I'm not with it,' said Bruce, somewhat perplexed.

'The black eye,' Delia spoke in a subdued tone as she looked towards the door.

'The black eye?' Bruce asked.

'Tina's,' replied Delia.

'I didn't notice,' said Bruce. It would appear that his mind that morning had been so filled with other subjects that he had been completely oblivious of the very visible injury sustained by one of the secretaries.

'Incredible,' continued Delia. 'You never noticed! It's not the first time, a present from her boyfriend! He has a history of violence and yet she won't give him up. The last time she asked to discuss the problem with me, I pointed out that she should consider her position very carefully. If he treats her like this now, what is likely to happen when they get married? Mind you, it's not all on one side. Tina can be a fiery little bitch when she wants to and as you know, women will batter verbally while men prefer to use their fists.'

Bruce listened intently and then decided to contribute to the conversation. 'To be honest, Delia,' he interjected, 'I feel sorry for Tina but I really thought that you were referring to a much more important matter – namely, the shooting.'

'The shooting?' repeated Delia, questioningly.

'Yes, surely you've heard about the gamekeeper's son up at the Hackford Hall estate who pointed a rifle at his mother and shot her in cold blood.'

'Not Jake Fenn again?' she asked.

'Exactly,' said Bruce.

'I know that little bounder,' Delia went on. 'Now something will have to be done. He didn't kill her, did he?'

'Fortunately not, but the injuries were enough to put his mother in hospital. I mentioned it, Delia, because when the time comes, it looks as if we shall need a full background history from you. And now I need a coffee. I must go and ask Tina to get me one. Are you joining me?'

'Of course,' replied Delia and grinned knowingly. She understood that Bruce really wanted to satisfy his curiosity by witnessing Tina's injury himself.

As Bruce opened the door and entered the outer office to make his request, the little boy who was being tested by Harry was passing through. All three secretaries looked up from their work.

'That's his third visit to the toilet,' remarked Sonia.

'I wonder what Dr Wilcox's doing to him?' Tina remarked with a grin at Bruce and in no way trying to disguise her black eye. In fact, of the two, Bruce was probably the most embarrassed as he pretended not to notice Tina's injury.

Just then Harry appeared at the door of his office. 'I'm worried,' he remarked. 'That young man has an unquenchable thirst.'

'So we noticed,' said Donna.

'It could be that he is just thirsty, but there may be an underlying reason.' Harry walked to the waiting area where Mrs Parker, the child's mother, was busy reading a magazine.

'Excuse me, Mrs Parker,' Harry enquired, 'is Scott normally as thirsty as this?'

'Not normally,' replied the child's mother. 'But now you say so, I have noticed that during the last few days, he keeps coming into the kitchen for a drink of water.'

Harry pondered for a moment and then said, 'We've now completed the testing session. Scott can stay here and you and I can have a little chat about the results.'

By this time the child had returned and was given a book to read in the waiting area whilst his mother was interviewed by Harry.

The assessment had uncovered some interesting points.

First Scott was a child of exceptionally high intelligence. His abilities, both verbal and non-verbal, fell well within the superior range. Despite this, however, at the age of eight years he had made little progress in spelling and reading. Further diagnostic tests showed that Scott had a poor short-term memory, especially for simple geometric shapes, like letters. Besides this, Harry had found that the child was cross-lateral. He wrote with his right hand but sighted with his left eye. When Scott was given a kaleidoscope to look through, he automatically put it up to his left eye.

Harry explained the problem to Scott's mother, pointing out that the child had exceptionally high intelligence but unfortunately had a learning difficulty with written language. The problem, he said, was often called 'dyslexia', or the fashionable term then being used, 'specific learning difficulties'. Harry enquired whether there was anyone else in the family with a spelling or a reading problem.

'I can't spell myself,' admitted Mrs Parker. 'I was never any good at school. Even today my husband always fills out the forms.'

'Dyslexia often runs in families,' said Harry, 'but you mustn't necessarily see it as a brain defect or something wrong with your brain. It's very often a brain difference. Famous people of very high intelligence, famous engineers, painters and scientists are often dyslexic and the truth is that Scott has very high intelligence. The Americans would call him a conundrum child. On the one hand, Scott is highly intelligent and on the other hand, he has a learning problem. What I am going to do is to ring Scott's head teacher and explain the situation, and I will ask if she can arrange some special remedial help in spelling and reading.'

'Thank you,' said Mrs Parker.

'And now,' Harry continued, 'the little question of Scott's unquenchable thirst. I feel that this should be investigated further.'

'But I took him to the doctor's a few days ago when he was complaining about stomach pains,' interrupted Mrs Scott.

'Did your doctor take a specimen of his urine?' enquired Harry.

'I don't think so,' replied Mrs Parker.

'Who is your doctor?' asked Harry.

'Dr Payne,' replied Mrs Parker.

'Oh yes, he is in the same practice as Dr Patel,' said Harry and he picked up the phone and spoke to his friend, Harjit Patel.

Harjit listened to Harry's description of Scott's persistent thirst. 'An obvious condition which springs to mind is diabetes,' he commented. Harry tried to muffle the phone for fear of alarming the child's mother if she heard.

'Can Mrs Parker and Scott come and see you?' asked Harry.

'Tell them to come immediately,' replied Harjit Patel.

Harry put the phone down and informed Mrs Parker that it would be sensible to take Scott to the surgery immediately.

That afternoon, whilst in the middle of writing reports, Harry received a phone call from Harjit Patel. 'Well done, Harry,' he said. 'You did us all a favour, especially the little boy. When we came to check his urine, it was saturated with sugar. It certainly looks like diabetes. He's now been admitted to the diabetic ward in Tanner Hospital and his parents will be given counselling. So, give yourself a pat on the back! Meanwhile George Payne, his doctor, has a very red face!'

As Harry put the phone down, he muttered to himself, 'Poor kid, a double frustration – first dyslexia and now diabetes.'

Chapter Eight
The Baverstone Ball Game

Bruce was well into his second term in Monaston by the time any light appeared on the horizon with regard to the house transfer. Another more reliable buyer had been found for the Whitfords' own residence and they had at last reached an agreement concerning the purchase of the four-bedroom house in Hatley.

It was mid-morning on Shrove Tuesday. Bruce had just arrived at his office. He noted a memo marked 'Urgent' on top of his in-tray. It was a request to phone the solicitor concerning the house. Within seconds he was through to the solicitor who was able to give him a definite date of when the contracts could be exchanged. Elated, Bruce rang his wife with the news.

'The local authority has agreed to give me three days off for moving house,' he told Marie. 'This is apparently the norm.' As he spoke, Bruce drew lines in his diary through the appropriate days.

After the short and animated conversation with his wife, Bruce then turned to more mundane tasks of reading letters and signing reports. He had hardly begun when Sarah Craig knocked on his door. Bruce knew that that afternoon they were both involved in a case in the neighbouring town of Baverstone. Although Sarah looked somewhat concerned and probably had something important to say, Bruce could not contain himself following the news about the house transfer.

'Within three weeks the whole family will be living here permanently,' he said. 'Our contract date has been arranged.'

'I'm delighted for you,' Sarah smiled and added, 'wonderful news. Now there's a little matter concerning this afternoon.'

'Don't worry, everything's under control,' Bruce interrupted.

'Oh, you are aware of the situation?' Sarah asked.

'Aware?' Bruce asked.

'Didn't you know it's Shrove Tuesday?' said Sarah.

'Yes,' replied Bruce. 'And tomorrow is Ash Wednesday, a day of obligation for us Catholics.'

'Don't you know what happens on Shrove Tuesday in Baverstone?' Sarah went on.

'No, should I?' asked Bruce.

'All Hell is let loose,' she said. 'It's the Baverstone ball game and I didn't realise until I read about it in the local paper last night.'

'A football match?' Bruce queried.

Sarah hardly had time to reply when Harry Wilcox poked his head round the door waving a referral form which had been wrongly placed in his own in-tray. 'This one belongs to you, Bruce. Sorry!'

'Thanks,' replied Bruce, adding, 'before you go, Harry, I thought you might like to know that a definite date has been arranged for the exchange of contracts so I shall be away for a few days moving house. I've obtained special permission from the authority. I will give you the dates later.'

'Good for you,' replied Harry.

'Sarah is just enlightening me about the so-called Baverstone ball game,' Bruce added.

Harry stopped in his tracks. 'Ah yes, of course. It's today, Shrove Tuesday,' he remarked, 'quite an historic event. Do you know anything about it?'

'Totally ignorant,' said Bruce. Harry paused. He could not miss the opportunity to air his knowledge of local history.

'The Baverstone ball game,' he began, 'goes back to the Middle Ages and some say possibly to the time of the Druids. In fact, it's put Baverstone on the map. It's not like your normal football match, Bruce, with your offsides and no fouling. In fact, the only rule is mob rule. So beware – avoid Baverstone on Shrove Tuesday!'

'But we can't,' Bruce responded. 'Sarah and I have a case over there.'

'Oh,' muttered Harry with a concerned air. 'Well, make sure your cars are in safe places and if you are going to watch, keep away from the ball. The ball is quite heavy, more like a medicine ball. It used to be made by the local saddler. They say the game was even rougher in the old days when the miners wore their pit boots,' Harry continued. 'The game normally goes up and down Long Street. It starts at three o'clock when a well-known personality, a footballer, boxer or perhaps a comedian throws the ball to the crowd from the window of the Golden Lion. I believe this year Benny Gayton is going to do the honours. The crowd usually likes the personality in question to come outside and have a kick.'

'Incidentally,' Harry went on, 'the Baverstone ball game is usually an opportunity for rival gangs to have a go at each other. At the moment it's the Burgesses versus the Millichips.'

'The name Burgess rings a bell,' interrupted Bruce. 'Liam Burgess is the name of the young man we are going to see. He hasn't got the best of records, shoplifting and truancy. I've been asked to do a court report on him. Sarah hasn't had much luck in stopping his truancy and we are contemplating making a recommendation for residential schooling, which should please the magistrates.'

'Well, there you are,' said Harry. 'Have a good ball game!' and he disappeared back to his office.

With the news that Liam Burgess would probably be participating in the ball game, Sarah rang his headmaster and arranged to bring the interview forward by half an hour. They would both travel across to Baverstone in Sarah's car and leave it in the school car park where it should be safe enough.

Within an hour, Bruce had completed most of his correspondence and consumed a quick sandwich and coffee, and he met up again with Sarah in the Town Hall car park as arranged, and the two of them set off on their journey. It was a dry if somewhat cloudy day as they arrived in the little market town of Baverstone. The main street, known as Long Street, was busy with shopkeepers boarding up their premises to protect themselves from broken windows and other damage.

'They certainly take it seriously,' remarked Bruce.

'Yes,' replied Sarah. 'The shopkeepers over here have mixed feelings about the ball game. Some would like to see an end to it, complaining that they lose the best part of a day's trade, while others see it as a way of putting Baverstone on the map and so bringing in trade. There's no doubt about it, a lot of outsiders come here on Shrove Tuesday. There will also be a police presence and the St John's Ambulance crew will be around later. There's another point – a collection for charity takes place on the day. They usually raise a lot of money to support the local children's home.

As they drove into the car park of Baverstone High School, the whole atmosphere seemed to be remarkably quiet. The car park itself was nearly empty and the school, which normally at lunchtime would be a hive of activity, was remarkably quiet.

'Is this the lull before the storm?' asked Bruce.

'Oh, didn't you know the school is practically empty? The children have a half-day holiday when the ball game is on,' replied Sarah. 'Ted Hughes, the head teacher, has arranged for you to test Liam in the staff room which will be empty and I can interview his mother in the head's office. As far as I know, the father will not be there. He left the scene some time ago.'

Within minutes Sarah and Bruce were exchanging pleasantries with Mrs Burgess and her son who were already sitting in the waiting area. Hearing the conversation, Ted Hughes, the head teacher, soon joined them. Like most of the Burgesses, Liam had dark hair, blue eyes and a lively podgy face. He was dressed in a T-shirt, jeans and trainers. No doubt prepared for the ball game, thought Bruce.

'Well, if we start now, Liam,' suggested Bruce, 'you will be in plenty of time for action later on.'

Liam grinned and readily followed Bruce to the nearby staff room while Sarah and Mrs Burgess were welcomed into the head teacher's office.

It didn't take long for Liam to become involved in the testing. Bruce soon noted that the boy demonstrated a remarkable aptitude for tasks which demanded spatial and constructional skills. From these, Bruce deduced that Liam, who like so many in the area came from an underprivileged background, probably had above-average intellectual potential. However, when tasks such as reading and spelling were involved, Liam became somewhat dispirited.

'Don't you enjoy reading?' Bruce enquired after a time, realising that Liam's literacy level was very low for his age.

'I hate it,' replied Liam.

'Tell me why,' suggested Bruce.

'Well, to begin with, the words never seem to stop still. When I look at that page, it looks like a waterfall.'

'Have you ever mentioned this to anyone before?' asked Bruce.

'No one's ever bothered to ask me,' replied Liam.

By this time Bruce had deduced that Liam was suffering from a degree of scotopic sensitivity syndrome. This is a particular form of visual dyslexia and is caused by the glare effect of black print on a white background. For some, the print may seem to move around, for others, it becomes distorted. The reader may have great difficulty in locating the spaces between words or passing from one line of print to the next. Children suffering from scotopic sensitivity do not realise that they see print differently from other children.

This was not the first time that Bruce had come across the condition. He recalled a case where a little girl had told him that words on a page seemed to wriggle like Elvis, whilst another had complained that words appeared like little insects jumping around on a page. Since taking an interest in scotopic sensitivity, Bruce had also learnt that the condition could be alleviated by the use of coloured lenses or tinted overlays on a page. Accordingly, he reached into his case and brought out a set of acetate overlays of a variety of colours. After experimenting with a few, Liam settled for a dark green overlay.

'This one really makes the print clear for me,' he remarked with a beam. 'The words don't jump around any more.'

'Good,' replied Bruce. 'In future I shall ask your teachers if you may use it whenever you have to read. Just put it over the print and you will find that you will be able to read much more easily.'

Bruce continued with the testing. As he suspected, Liam's learning difficulty was even more complicated. Besides suffering from a form of visual dyslexia, he had a very low sequencing ability, in other words, he had great difficulty in putting a series of sounds together in their correct order. Such a skill is essential for the mastery of spelling and reading.

Poor child, thought Bruce. No wonder he's turned to antisocial activities.

After the session was over, Bruce carefully returned his equipment to its case and then took Liam back to the head teacher's office. The time was fast approaching three o'clock and the hubbub of a gathering crowd could be heard in Long Street. Ted Hughes, the head teacher, recognised that Liam was anxious to join in the fray. 'If we let you go, Liam, will you promise not to smuggle the ball?'

Liam grinned. 'Yes, sir, I promise,' he replied.

'Go on then,' said Ted and off the boy went.

'Do you understand what I meant by smuggling the ball?' Ted asked Bruce as he invited him to take a seat in his office.

'Not quite,' replied Bruce.

'Well, smuggling the ball is a common practice in the ball game out there. A group gets together and tries to keep the ball and hide it. The practice is acceptable towards the end of the game but not at the beginning. In some years a group of spoilsports have tried to get it right at the start of the game and this has ruined the whole afternoon for the rest. The tradesmen particularly object if this happens. Rightly so; they feel that all the preparation they have put into the event is wasted. Anyway, we're not here to talk about the ball game but really what we are going to do about lazy Liam. What is your verdict, Mr Whitford?' the head teacher enquired as he sat at his desk.

Bruce paused and drew breath. Why did Ted Hughes use the term 'lazy Liam'?

'First,' Bruce began and looked over at Mrs Burgess who was sitting next to Sarah Craig in front of the head's desk, 'your son, Liam, has plenty of intelligence. Don't you agree,

Mrs Burgess?'

The child's mother nodded in agreement.

'But,' continued Bruce, 'did you know that he has a serious learning difficulty when it comes to spelling and reading?' Bruce looked questioningly at the head teacher.

'I've always seen Liam as a lazy speller,' remarked Ted Hughes.

'You might see him as a lazy speller,' continued Bruce, 'but the truth is that Liam not only has great difficulty in writing and spelling but when he looks at a sheet of writing, he doesn't see it in the same way as you and I do. In fact, to use his words, "the letters seem to dance around and the whole page looks like a waterfall".'

'A waterfall?' repeated the head teacher.

'It's not an uncommon condition,' Bruce continued. 'It's sometimes referred to as the scotopic sensitivity syndrome and it arises from the glare effect of black print on a white background. The glare or contrast has the effect of distorting the print for some children and of course for adults as well. Some describe it as fuzzy. Others say that the words seem to move around and in some cases they actually seem to jump. I remember one child who read the word "heart" as "earth". What had happened was that the "h" at the beginning appeared to have jumped to the end of the word. Scotopic sensitivity is like a kind of photophobia. People wear dark glasses to reduce the glare effect in bright sunlight; similarly by using tinted lenses or coloured overlays such as these,' Bruce produced the tinted acetates from his case, 'you can reduce the glare effect. Liam found the dark green overlay particularly helpful.'

Ted Hughes, Sarah Craig and Mrs Burgess all listened intently as Bruce continued to explain Liam's learning difficulty. Each began to see the child from another viewpoint, especially when Bruce pointed out that recent research in the United States had highlighted the fact that some fifty per cent of juvenile delinquents had been found to suffer from a form of dyslexia.

'Imagine the situation,' Bruce said. 'Year after year you fail at school. Despite having normal intelligence, you have great difficulty in doing what other children seem to find easy, namely learning to read and write. Not surprisingly you become confused. You are told that you are lazy or stupid or thick, and so you begin to believe it yourself. So what happens? Some children retreat into themselves. They become withdrawn. Others turn to antisocial activities. They become young criminals. They play truancy and get their kicks out of shoplifting and so on. Don't think that I'm trying to excuse Liam for his misdemeanours but there is another side to the child. I shall write this up in my report.'

As Bruce paused, the excitement outside in Long Street had reached a climax. The town clock struck three as a thousand voices shrieked with delight and numerous pairs of hands reached skywards as the gaily-ribboned ball was tossed from the upper window of the Golden Lion Inn by the comedian, Benny Gayton. As the 1972 Baverstone ball game began the sun pushed its way to the front of the dark clouds to see what was going on in that little market town.

'It looks as if the ball game has begun,' remarked Ted Hughes. 'Are you going to join in today?'

'Well, I would like to have a look at the event without becoming too involved,' replied Bruce.

'If you want to keep out of danger, I would suggest that you position yourself on the canal side of Long Street – but not too near the canal,' Ted added with a grin, 'or you might find yourself in the water with the ball.'

Having paid their respects to the headmaster and Mrs Burgess, Bruce and Sarah made their way back to the car park where they deposited their working equipment in the car and then proceeded towards a spot near the canal from which the game could be observed comfortably a little way away from the main crowd. Even at that distance, however, the atmosphere would at times become contagious as the ball was periodically kicked in their direction. The shouting rose in a crescendo when Benny Gayton himself had a kick at the ball. Unlike another famous comedian who had started the game in the 1930s and thereafter sought refuge in a shop, Benny had been persuaded to venture out and participate in the event and he was clearly enjoying it.

On another occasion following a scrummage, a young man found himself at the bottom of a pile of bodies, and he yelled that his back was broken. Within no time members of the St John's Ambulance Brigade were on the scene. However, it appeared to be a false alarm and the boy made a good recovery and joined in the game once more. Yet another false alarm occurred when a little girl shrieked as she was squashed against a wall by the surging crowd, but again no serious injury appeared to have occurred.

For the next twenty minutes, the ball was kicked to and fro from one end of Long Street to the other. Then unexpectedly, while Sarah was busy pointing out members of the families she recognised, the ball came hurtling towards them. It in fact went over their heads and straight into the canal. Pandemonium reigned as gangs of youths poured down towards the area where Bruce and Sarah had hitherto been enjoying an otherwise peaceful view. Within seconds, their safety seemed threatened.

'They're not from around here,' yelled a young hooligan who happened to be one of the Millichip brothers, pointing at Bruce and Sarah. 'Give them a dip in the canal!' For a brief period, attention was diverted from the ball, which was now spinning in the water, to the two apparently harmless but well-dressed observers. Bruce and Sarah felt both outnumbered and trapped, and were about to defend themselves as best they could, when out of the blue appeared Liam Burgess.

'Stop them, Les!' he yelled to his older brother. 'Those people are friends of mine and Mum's.'

Les Burgess was a stocky, muscular young man of about six foot, whose hobby was body-building. He was employed as a bouncer in a neighbouring town. Few would tangle with him when he was around and now he had members of his gang to support him. Within seconds, what could have been a nasty incident was averted and Bruce and Sarah escaped unscathed. The sight of Les Burgess with some of his cohorts was enough to dissuade the hooligans from assaulting the couple and attention was again focused on the ball.

As some youths prepared to wade into the canal to retrieve the prized possession, Bruce and Sarah, still intact but somewhat ruffled, decided to beat a hasty retreat.

'I must make a point of thanking Liam Burgess for getting us out of what could have been a nasty situation,' Bruce remarked.

'Don't worry. I will phone the school tomorrow and tell Ted Hughes what a good boy he was,' replied Sarah. She asked, 'What are you going to do now?'

'Go back to my digs, I suppose, and write up the report on Liam. It's a bit late to return to the office,' replied Bruce.

'True,' said Sarah. 'Only it's Shrove Tuesday and you know what happens on Shrove Tuesdays besides the Baverstone ball game?'

Bruce reflected and then exclaimed, 'Pancakes!'

'Exactly,' replied Sarah and added, 'Why don't we go back to my flat and make some?'

The invitation caught Bruce by surprise but it sounded good to him so he readily agreed. Before long, they were back in Monaston. Sarah dropped Bruce off at the car park to collect his car and he then followed her out to the Butterworth Road where her flat, one of two in a large residential house, was located. Bruce noted that it was much more spacious than his own little bedsit near the town centre where he had been living for almost three months now.

'Have you ever made pancakes, or do you leave it to your wife?' enquired Sarah as she invited Bruce into the kitchen, which also had a dining area.

'Actually I have in the past,' replied Bruce, and he paused and added, 'If I remember rightly, the basic ingredients are milk, eggs, flour and of course, a pinch of salt.'

'You have made them,' remarked Sarah. 'My mother taught me always to rub a little butter around the edge of the pan – it pays off – and always serve them hot.'

Before long the two of them were watching the sizzling pancakes and practising tossing them in the pan. Along with a cup of tea, they soon consumed three pancakes each and were busy mulling over the day's escapade in Baverstone when the phone rang. Sarah went to the hall to answer it.

The phone call appeared to be a serious one and it took a long time. There were periods when Sarah seemed to be doing nothing but listening. Occasionally she would make a remark such as, 'Do you think it will work out?' and 'We've discussed this before.' After a while, Bruce thought it would be politic to take advantage of the interval by cleaning the dishes. He was drying the last plate when Sarah returned.

'Sorry about the time,' she said. 'That was a long distance call from my husband in America.'

'Oh, he's keeping tabs on you,' said Bruce with a smile.

'You might say that,' replied Sarah in a resigned manner and added, 'Actually he wants me to pack in my job here and go out to the States.'

'Are you going to?' asked Bruce with obvious concern.

'I have mixed feelings and I'm totally confused,' Sarah admitted, 'but I think I shall probably give way and try to pick up the pieces of my marriage.' As she spoke, Bruce noticed a tear in her eye.

There was a brief silence in which both stared at each other in embarrassment and then Bruce said, 'I shall miss you. I am sure the whole office will.' He knew that the last thing he wanted was for Sarah to leave, but it would be wrong even for him to comment on the situation. Basically it was her own personal problem which she had to work out for herself.

Another embarrassing silence followed and Bruce again broke it. 'Well, the pancakes were a nice finale to the ball game. I suppose I ought to go and do this wretched report now,' and he prepared to go. As they went to the door, Bruce put his arm on Sarah's shoulder. 'Cheer up,' he said. 'Things are bound to work out.'

'Thanks for doing the dishes!' Sarah called as they waved goodbye and Bruce climbed into his car and drove back towards the town centre.

As he drove away, Bruce couldn't help but ponder on his last statement to Sarah that things were bound to work out. Did he really want things to work out between her and her husband? He certainly would have preferred her to stay in Monaston rather than go to America. Que sera, sera, he thought to himself.

Since there was no telephone available in his accommodation, Bruce broke his journey to make a quick call to his family. His daughter, Josie, answered. 'Mummy's tossing pancakes!' she shrieked.

Bruce could hear the noise of other excited children in the background. Soon, however, his wife, Marie came to the phone.

'Hello, dear,' she said. 'You certainly pick your moments to call.'

'I gather you're making pancakes,' Bruce remarked.

'What else on Shrove Tuesday?' Marie replied. 'Aren't

you jealous?'

'Of course,' Bruce answered. 'Do you think you could keep some for me when I come at the weekend?'

'It's not a thing you can keep,' said Marie. 'Anyway, if you really feel neglected, I will make you some at the weekend.'

Bruce felt a twinge of guilt as the subject of pancakes was pursued. He did not think it was wise to enlighten Marie about how he had spent the last two hours and for the rest of the call he steered the conversation to other areas.

When Bruce arrived at the office the next day he could not help but notice two ladies in the waiting area wearing rather provocative clothes, bedecked with jewellery and both sporting Mohican haircuts. The surprise on his face was still apparent as he entered the main office, where he soon sensed an undercurrent of apparent amusement. 'Who are they?' Bruce enquired in a whisper, looking at Tina.

'The tall one is Tiger Royale. Dr Wilcox is at present testing her son, Tex Royale,' Tina replied in a low voice. 'The other one is her friend and business partner. You can guess the kind of business,' she added, looking knowingly at Bruce. 'The friend is nicknamed Bungalow because they say she has nothing upstairs.' Tina grinned. 'We've just had a bit of a laugh,' she continued, 'because Donna has just spoken to her and called her Mrs Bungalow, thinking that it was her real name. Fortunately she didn't seem to feel insulted.'

'I like it,' Bruce remarked.

'By the way, Mr Whitford, did you enjoy the ball game yesterday?' enquired Irene Cathcart.

'Interesting and a bit terrifying at one point,' replied Bruce.

'It wasn't you who smuggled the ball then?' Irene continued.

Two ladies wearing rather provocative clothes and both sporting Mohican haircuts.

'Well, actually I didn't stay until the end – thought it was safer to get out while I could before I ended up in the canal!' Bruce grinned and went into his room.

About twenty minutes later, while Bruce was still going through his correspondence, Harry knocked on the door. Sipping a mug of coffee, he remarked, 'A heavy cloud of suspicion is still over your head, Bruce. After all, who else could it be?'

Bruce looked puzzled. 'I'm not with it,' he retorted.

'Surely you've read the local rag?' Harry asked.

Bruce was still bemused. 'I'm afraid that you will have to enlighten me,' he said.

'Didn't you hear?' replied Harry. 'They smuggled the ball from the ball game into the Council House, here in fact. No one seems to know how; it was found last night beside the information desk in a brown cardboard box addressed to the mayor. It was a suspicious-looking box. Even the police were involved before it was opened.'

Bruce stared in disbelief. He now appreciated the remarks made earlier by Irene, the secretary. 'Oh,' he smiled, 'and they think it was me, no doubt aided and abetted by Sarah Craig who was also at the ball game.'

'You will no doubt have to produce alibis at some point,' said Harry, still affecting an air of seriousness. 'Arthur has already produced his.' Harry was, of course, alluding to Arthur Brown, the office jester.

There was a short silence and then Bruce, continuing in the same spirit, remarked, 'At least I don't interview ladies of ill repute.'

Harry immediately realised that Bruce was referring to Tiger Royale and her sidekick. 'Consider yourself lucky that the Royale family are not on your patch,' he said. 'They've given me a great deal of stress over the years,' he muttered, looking out of the window and still sipping his coffee. 'Anyway, I've now persuaded Tiger, who was once known as Rita Stubbs before she changed her name by deed poll, to accept a residential placement for young Tex.'

Spotting the opportunity to slip an interesting ambiguity into the conversation, Bruce interjected, 'By the way, Harry, what do you recommend when you come across a left-handed hooker?'

Harry paused and then replied, 'I take it that you are referring to a left-handed child who has not been taught properly how to hold a pencil or position his paper.'

'Exactly,' replied Bruce.

'Well,' continued Harry, 'I use the standard guidance sheets for left-handers but, of course, it depends a lot on the age of the child. If he has already developed an unorthodox writing posture, however cramped, it may be too ingrained to change. Anyway, whilst on the subject of sinistrality,' here Harry deliberately used the more sophisticated term for left-handedness, 'I want to show you something.'

He disappeared back to his room and returned seconds later, brandishing a book on classical art. 'Look here,' he said, pointing to a glossy picture of a sculpture. 'What do you see?'

Bruce examined the plate carefully and replied, 'As it says below, it's a picture of the famous male nude by Rodin.'

'Exactly,' retorted Harry. 'But do you notice anything in particular?'

'I'm afraid not,' said Bruce.

'Well, if you look closely,' Harry continued, 'you will see that his right testicle is lower than the left.'

'So what?' Bruce responded with a mixture of surprise and amusement.

Harry continued, 'As well as being dyslexic, Rodin was known to be left-handed. It is generally believed that the sculpture you are looking at was a mirror image of himself.

Some tentative research has suggested that males who are naturally left-handed usually have the right testicle lower than the left one.'

Bruce reflected and muttered, 'Interesting, if it is true.'

'And do you see the implications?' Harry asked. 'One of the problems which many parents have with very young children is deciding which is the dominant or preferred hand. Now, if research confirms that left-handed males normally have a right testicle which is lower than the left, this might be a warning to those confused parents who sometimes try to force their child into using his right hand. The problem is – how do we do the research?'

Bruce looked at Harry a little mystified, and after a few seconds remarked, 'The implications could be serious, as long as it doesn't turn out to be a cock and bull story that is.'

'Very droll, Bruce,' replied Harry, and he made one of his characteristic prompt exits.

Hardly had Bruce settled back to checking and signing his reports and letters when there was a knock at the door. It was Jesse Fry, the education welfare officer.

'What can I do for you, Jesse?' asked Bruce with a smile.

'I won't keep you,' replied Jesse, 'but you may be interested to know that last night we had a phone call out of the blue from our long lost son Tommy.'

'Great news!' exclaimed Bruce.

'This was the first time we have spoken to him for two years,' said Jesse. 'Not surprisingly my wife broke down in tears. Tommy seems to be well; he is still painting the sides of ships. But listen to this: he has apparently begun a relationship with a Japanese lady. He says that he will be bringing her up here to Monaston in the not too distant future. They intend to get married and then move out to Tokyo to live there.'

Bruce listened intently to these disclosures, noting in

particular Jesse's last statement concerning Japan. 'If they do go out to Japan,' he remarked, 'it may not be a bad thing. Japan is a highly-structured society and people with Asperger's Syndrome, like Tommy, often flourish in such an environment.

'In view of their relationship problems, they find it harder to get along in an open society, such as ours, where there is so much freedom. So it might work.'

'Well, I hope so,' said Jesse and added, 'Thanks again for all the support you have given us in the past. I will keep you posted,' and with that he left.

Whilst Bruce had been busy talking to Jesse, Harry Wilcox had left the office and was on his way to see a seven-year-old girl at Mutley Infants School. The girl had been referred to the SPS on account of behavioural difficulties. She rejoiced in the name of Amber Potter and was reported to be very bright but rather manipulative and dogmatic. Harry had left early for his appointment in order to give himself time to make a slight detour to change a tyre on his car.

Until now he had left the changing of car tyres to the garage he normally used but recently he had learnt that it could be more economic and expedient to have tyres changed at Fast-Fitters, a small specialist business set up in a back street near the town centre. When Harry arrived, there was already a car jacked up on the forecourt with a young man working on it.

'I shall be with you in a few seconds,' he shouted to Harry.

'No hurry,' replied Harry as he watched the young man change the back tyres of a Ford Cortina. He was impressed with the speed and dexterity employed by the young man at his job.

Within a short time the job had been completed and Harry had had his own tyre checked and changed.

'You don't recognise me, do you Dr Wilcox?' the young man remarked.

'You don't recognise me, do you, Dr Wilcox?' the young man remarked as he looked up and smiled, whilst adjusting the air pressure on the new tyre.

Harry, taken aback by the remark, looked at him questioningly. Although he did not recognise him he felt that it would not be politic to admit it completely. 'Your face is familiar,' he said.

'My name is Freddie Busby,' the young man replied. 'I was always in trouble at school and eventually you managed to get me a place down south in a boarding school. I was there for three years and they sorted me out and now I am running my own tyre business.'

Harry gazed at the young man. 'Freddy Busby,' he repeated as memories came flooding back. 'Weren't you suspended from the Alderman Brown School on a number of occasions?'

The young man grinned and replied, 'Three times to be exact.' He then added, 'You certainly need a new tyre here. I've checked the other three. The front offside one will need changing in the near future.'

'I shall be back to see you then,' said Harry. As he drove away, Harry had a feeling of satisfaction that he had contributed to the reform of yet another deviant. Work was certainly the answer. At least young Freddy seemed to be on the straight and narrow at the moment, although there had been a time when most had despaired of him.

Mrs Milson, the head teacher of Mutley Infants, was a gentle, elderly lady. She welcomed Harry into her office and invited him to use it for the assessment of the pupil whom she had referred. 'I'll go and fetch Amber now,' she said with some trepidation in her voice. 'You may find that she is a little awkward. We've had a lot of problems with her. Her mother is coming in to see you later.'

As he set up his test equipment on the head teacher's desk as usual, Harry wondered what he had let himself in for; the child's extremely problematic reputation had preceded her. However, he was an experienced psychologist and over the years had acquired a wide repertoire of techniques for enlisting the co-operation of both children and adults. Soon he heard footsteps and voices outside the room and the door opened.

'Here we are, Amber,' said Mrs Milson. 'This is Dr Wilcox. He's come to see you.'

The little girl fixed her gaze on Harry as if weighing him up. She paused and then remarked, 'What do I need a doctor for? I'm not ill.'

By this time Mrs Milson had left the room, beating a hasty retreat.

'Of course, you're not ill,' replied Harry. 'In fact, you're in perfect health. I've just come along to see how you are getting on with your schoolwork. We have lots of interesting things to do. Look, here are some puzzles,' he said, pointing at some small boxes on the desk, 'all sorts of interesting things. Now, let's see if you can sit on this chair and show me how clever you are.' He helped Amber to sit on a chair which was adjacent to his own. He always preferred this arrangement since sitting a child directly opposite, he felt, could contribute to a confrontational approach.

'Now, dear,' began Harry.

Amber again looked him straight in the eye and, unimpressed with the apparently ingratiating remark, replied, 'Don't you "dear" me.' Harry began to realise that this was not going to be the easiest of interviews. Pretending to ignore the remark, he drew Amber's attention to the pieces of a puzzle which he had arranged in front of her.

'See here,' he said. 'See if you can make an animal out of these.'

Amber obliged and within seconds had completed the puzzle. It was perfect but upside-down in relation to herself.

'Very good,' remarked Harry, 'but it's upside-down.'

Amber looked at the completed shape and replied, 'Not for someone sitting opposite.'

'Absolutely,' said Harry with a beam and proceeded to the next task.

It was not long before Harry realised that he was dealing with a child of exceptional ability. Everything he put in front of her she completed quickly and easily, and often with a look of disdain. After about thirty minutes, Amber began to betray signs of boredom.

'How long is this going on for?' she asked.

'We've almost finished,' Harry replied apologetically. 'I just want you to do a little reading and some sums. Try this one,' he said, trying to inject as much enthusiasm into the situation as possible. 'If I gave you three sweets and your mummy gave you three more, how many would you have altogether?'

Judging by her previous responses, Harry was sure that Amber would have little difficulty with the problem. However, on this occasion she surprisingly took her time and after due thought came out with the very definite answer, 'Eight!'

'Are you sure?' Harry asked.

'Perfectly,' the little girl replied. 'Do you want me to prove it?'

'Go on,' replied Harry.

'Well, give me a pencil and paper,' she said.

Harry duly obliged and then proceeded to watch the child write a figure three on the paper and then join it to a mirror image of the same to complete the figure eight. 'There you are,' she said. 'One three and another three make eight.'

'Very good,' Harry remarked, and added, 'There's no doubt that you have lots and lots of brains.'

The child stared at him questioningly and replied, 'As far as I know, I only have one!'

By this time Harry was feeling a little awkward, if not to say embarrassed. He was relieved that the interview was coming to an end. When he worked out Amber's scores on the intelligence test, he was not surprised to discover that they fell well into the intellectually-gifted range. The child was also reading and writing many years ahead of her age level.

As is often the procedure, the testing session was followed by a counselling session with the child's mother and the head teacher and class teacher. Harry well appreciated the difficulties of having a child of exceptional ability in a normal classroom and a large one at that. Amber was one of thirty-five children. Not only was she extremely clever but she was awkward and didn't suffer fools gladly. She related poorly to other children in her class and they in turn disliked her.

'So what can we do about Amber?' Harry began the discussion which was held in the head teacher's office.

'You tell us,' replied Miss Ferris, the child's class teacher. 'She refuses to do her schoolwork, complaining that it's too easy, and she often won't join in games with the other children, saying they're too babyish.'

'I sympathise with you,' Harry replied. 'Believe me, I do. Amber co-operated reasonably well in the one-to-one situation as most children do, but even then she could be awkward. The problem with these children of high ability, or gifted children if you like, is that they have special needs, just as other children do at the lower end of the spectrum but, unfortunately, our educational system is not geared up to providing for them, despite the fact that these children will ultimately offer more to society than any other group. So catering for the needs of gifted children would make good economic sense.

'There's also another point,' Harry continued. 'If we ignore this group, some will turn their very real abilities into antisocial and even illegal activities. There are plenty of gifted criminals in society today.'

The rest of the group nodded at this last statement and Harry paused for a moment, thinking that he had pontificated enough.

At this point Mrs Milson joined the discussion. 'Can you suggest anything practical, Dr Wilcox, that we could do with Amber?'

'Well,' replied Harry, 'there is one thing we could try and that is putting her up into an older age group. This is not necessarily the answer for all children of high ability but it could be of some help in Amber's case for two reasons. First, the work could be more challenging and I think she needs this.'

Mrs Potter, Amber's mother, signalled her approval of Harry's suggestion. 'Yes,' she said. 'Amber's always complaining that she doesn't like school because the work is too easy but I do realise that it is hard for the teacher with such a big class to give her special work, so I'm trying to take an objectionable viewpoint.'

Harry, along with the others in the room tried to conceal any signs of amusement at the unintentional malapropism and continued, 'The pressure of being in a class of older children and the general expectations in such a group could, hopefully, make her less cocky and awkward. Maybe in such a situation she would conform more easily,' he concluded.

The suggested promotion of Amber to a higher class was discussed at length, and the group finally agreed that it was worth trying. Harry also made a further suggestion, namely that Amber's parents should join the local Group for Gifted Children, which had been set up in the Monaston area. The group provided the opportunity for children of high intelligence to mix socially with others of similar abilities and interests, and, in so doing, give them the chance of realising that they were not the only clever children around. In short, it could help them from developing a distorted view of their own importance.

As Harry drove back to the department late that afternoon, he felt reasonably satisfied with himself. At least he had been able to make some practical suggestions to help solve a rather awkward case. The proof of the pudding, of course, would be in the eating, he reflected.

During the few months that Bruce had lived in Monaston, he had been able to sample some of the borough's social and leisure amenities. At the invitation of Arthur Brown, he had joined a table tennis club, and he also visited the local swimming baths at least one evening during the week, again at Arthur's suggestion.

It was one evening, in late March, when both Bruce and Arthur, still dripping water, having completed a number of lengths of the bath, were intently watching a young girl in her early teens moving gracefully and rapidly through the water. Standing at the end of the bath, a man was timing her. 'She made me feel like a tugboat being passed by a speed boat,' said Bruce.

'I see Sarah has arrived,' Arthur remarked casually.

'Sarah who?' replied Bruce.

'Sarah Craig, of course,' said Arthur. 'She's just dived in up the far end. Here she comes.'

Sarah soon passed the two spectators, doing an impressive crawl. She then completed another length, doing the breast stroke. On this occasion she recognised both Bruce and Arthur on the side of the bath and shouted a brisk 'hello'.

After completing her second length, Sarah got out and joined the two men.

'What a figure!' Arthur muttered before she was in earshot.

'Exactly what I was thinking,' Bruce replied in a subdued voice.

'Well, what a surprise!' remarked Sarah as she arrived beside them. 'I've seen Arthur here before but not you, Bruce.'

'I usually come on Tuesdays. I now know I picked the wrong day,' Bruce replied.

At that moment, the young girl who was being timed by her father, passed them again. It could have been her twentieth length. 'She's dedicated,' Arthur remarked.

'Do you think so?' said Sarah, adding in a hushed voice, 'In actual fact, it is probably her dad who is dedicated.'

Both Bruce and Arthur looked questioningly at Sarah.

'Go on,' said Bruce.

'Well, believe it or not, that young lady is one of my cases. She's called Samantha Brace, and is known as Sammy. She swims for the county and she goes to Goose Common High, but that's not the end of the story,' continued Sarah in a low tone. 'Sammy has a very poor school attendance record. She has been found to be "wagging it", and it's generally believed that her father, who runs his own business, has an obsession about making her a swimming champion, and he takes her to various swimming baths around the Midlands during the week for extra training. She's also known to be down here most mornings around seven o'clock.

'The school is complaining that not only does Sammy miss important lessons which are going to affect her O level results but she is often very tired when she does attend them. Also the teachers believe that she is being pressurised into becoming a swimming champion and is doing heavy training mainly to please her father. I've discussed the case with the head of year at her school, whom I know, and we think that the best thing to do would be to refer her to the

SPS for an investigation.'

'Thanks,' said Bruce with a forced air of resignation, 'as Goose Green is on my patch, it's over to me.'

Sarah paused, then said, 'The school does need help, Bruce, in fact it's really the girl who needs help.'

'I can see it's going to be a tricky situation,' he replied, glancing up towards Sammy's father who, at that moment, appeared to be giving his daughter a lecture as she hung on to the rail at the end of the bath. 'Anyway, I've got a few days to think about it, I hope, before the referral comes through,' he added.

Sarah promised that Samantha Brace would be referred to the SPS, and the following Wednesday the referral, duly completed by the child's head teacher, was lying on his desk. It was not the first time that he had had to deal with an over-ambitious parent, and he knew that in such cases, considerable tact and diplomacy were called for. Initially he planned to visit the child at her school and administer a number of psychometric tests. This could offer a rough guide to Samantha's intellectual and academic potential. At the same time, it would be possible to discuss the child's interest in swimming with Samantha herself. This should help him ascertain whether the girl was really interested in doing well in swimming, and whether she considered that the endless hours of training were worthwhile.

Within a few days the interview was arranged and Bruce met Samantha at her school. Test results soon indicated that Samantha was a child of at least high or above-average ability and who, with hard work, was capable of obtaining passes in O level subjects. The interesting part, however, came when Bruce asked the child to tell him about her hobbies or pastimes. Samantha made it quite clear that there was no time in her life for leisure activities.

'If I'm not at school, I'm either eating, sleeping or swimming,' she replied in a voice which was less than enthusiastic.

There was a pause. Bruce questioned her, 'Swimming – you're interested in swimming?'

Samantha looked at him. 'Interested? I've been doing it since I was seven.'

'Do you enjoy it?' Bruce asked.

Samantha looked at the floor. 'Not really,' she replied.

'So why do you train so hard?' Bruce continued.

'Because my dad wants me to be a champion,' she said.

'And don't you want to be a champion?' asked Bruce. Samantha burst into tears.

Back at the education office, Bruce was busy considering strategies for helping Samantha. The situation was a sensitive one requiring considerable thought. He was still musing over the problem an hour later when he received an unexpected visit from Delia Berry.

'Hello Delia,' he greeted her. 'Just the person I want!'

Delia smiled. 'What can I do for you?' she asked.

Bruce then proceeded to tell Delia all about the interview with Samantha Brace, and how she had cried about her father's obsession with her reaching the dizzy heights.

Delia listened intently and then came to a very definite conclusion. 'Someone needs to explain to him quite clearly what he is doing to the poor girl and also that he is doing it for his own self-aggrandisement, not hers.'

'Exactly,' said Bruce, seizing the opportunity and realising that the answer to his problem was being laid on a plate. 'What we need is someone who can interview the father tactfully but firmly, who is reliable and persuasive and who is experienced in home visits.'

Delia spotted the trap but unlike a lesser mortal who would have immediately recoiled, she characteristically took on the challenge. 'You want me to do the home visit?' she queried.

'Would you?' replied Bruce with a feeling of relief. 'It

would be a great help. You could use my report to hide behind to some degree,' he added, 'and I am sure that the school will supply further written evidence to back the case up.'

It was mid-morning the following Wednesday when Bruce received a phone call from Delia Berry. She described in detail how she had visited the Brace family the evening before and how the problem appeared to have been solved. Although somewhat prickly and defensive at first, Samantha's father gradually came to agree that there should be a significant reduction in the amount of training the child should be subjected to and that Samantha should be encouraged to give more time to her academic studies and to socialise more with her peers. In fact, it was agreed that Samantha herself should dictate the amount of swimming she would do in the future. Delia reported that at the end of a long interview both the girl and her mother appeared visibly relieved.

'You've worked the miracle again, Delia!' exclaimed Bruce.

Delia put down the phone at her end with a self-satisfied smirk at having solved a case. Bruce, however, had little time to ponder over the good news. He knew that two ladies, both mothers of difficult children, had been in the waiting area some time. One had an appointment with Harry Wilcox and the other with Bruce himself.

Harry had already collected his client and as Bruce passed his office, he smiled knowingly as he heard Harry remark, 'You say that you have tried everything with Kevin, but Mrs Nesbit, have you tried anything properly? That is – seen it right through to the end?'

A few minutes later, by coincidence, Bruce found himself in a similar position to his colleague. He too had a parent whose retort to every suggestion he made regarding her recalcitrant child was, 'I've tried that and it doesn't work.'

Glancing at the pile of correspondence on his in-tray, Bruce noted that there, on the top, was a letter from a parish priest. By association he recalled the concluding line in Tennyson's *The Morte d'Arthur* which he had studied as a boy:

> More things are wrought by prayer
> Than this world dreams of.

In an air of resignation but partly with tongue in cheek, he asked the mother, 'Have you tried prayer?'

As she stared at him in apparent disbelief with glazed eyes, the single chime of a church bell could be heard in the distance. It was the Feast of Corpus Christi, a day of obligation.

Glossary

Ant to Zip

This is a highly-organised step-by-step programme for teaching reading, spelling and writing. It is particularly useful for those suffering from dyslexia; obtainable from GCIC 21, Hampton Lane, Solihull, B91 2QJ.

Asperger's Syndrome

This is a disorder characterised by some of the features of autism such as abnormalities of social interaction and repetitive and stereotyped interests and activities, but without the delay or retardation in language and intellectual development that is seen in true autism. Other characteristics include poor eye contact, a lack of empathy, little ability to form friendships, one-sided conversations, intense absorption in a special interest and clumsy movements.

Baverstone ball game

The parallel here is the famous Atherstone ball game which takes place every Shrove

Tuesday in the market town of Atherstone. It is an ancient and interesting game. The 'ball' is specially made each year and is 'thrown out' by a prominent sporting or show business personality. Shop windows are boarded up and traffic is diverted on the afternoon of Shrove Tuesday whilst the game, in which hundreds of people take part, progresses. The game can be traced back to the Middle Ages, and some say even to the Roman era.

Down's Syndrome   A congenital condition characterised by a flat skull, stubby fingers, an unusual pattern of skin folds on the palms of the hands and the soles of the feet, epicanthic folds on the eyelids, a fissured tongue and often severe mental retardation. The disorder is named from the British physician J.L.H. Down, who first described it in 1866. It is the single most common clinical condition with mental retardation as a primary symptom and occurs in approximately one out of every seven hundred births. The incidence is higher with elderly mothers.

Dysgraphia This refers to an inability to write properly. It is often associated with dyslexia.

Dyslexia This is basically a failure to master the mechanics of spelling and reading. It is always a spelling problem, since spelling requires different mental operation to reading, and it is frequently an arithmetic problem as well. Although often referred to as a specific learning difficulty, dyslexia is a very complex condition and can affect other aspects of life such as organisational skills.

Educational psychology This is a sub-discipline of psychology concerned with theories and problems in education. Educational psychologists normally have a long training (six to seven years). Qualification and experience in teaching is part of the training.

Education welfare officer At the time of writing this title still existed in certain areas of the country, although today it has been largely superseded by the title education social worker. The post is the successor of the school board officer appointed in the early

	part of the twentieth century to secure school attendance.
Elective mutism	This is sometimes referred to as 'selective mutism' and quite literally implies someone selecting not to speak. This is a childhood disorder and is characterised by a failure to speak in specific social situations where speech is expected, such as school. Normally the condition lasts only for a few months. Treatment can be carried out by a step-by-step programme which focuses directly on the child's reluctance to speak. Behaviour is shaped through rewards.
Benny Gayton	Similarities may be noted here with the popular real-life comedian Larry Grayson whose childhood was spent in Nuneaton and who never lost contact with the borough.
Las Meniñas (The Ladies in Waiting)	Sometimes regarded as the greatest painting in the world, it is certainly the most complex and intriguing of the portraits of Diego Velázquez. It can be seen in the Praedo Museum in Madrid.

Monaston   The name arises from its monastery foundation. cf. Nuneaton, which is reputed to have arisen from the foundation of a nunnery.

Monks   The Nuneaton football club is nicknamed the Nuns.

Munch, Edvard   Painter of the famous picture entitled *The Scream*.

Picasso, Pablo (1881-1973)   Spanish painter and one of the original exponents of Cubism in which objects were reduced to cubic and other geometric forms.

Plain English Campaign   Founded by Chrissie Maher of Liverpool in order to combat what is seen as the impenetrable waffle and gobbledegook of English bureaucracy.

Pneumoconiosis   A general name which is applied to a chronic form of inflammation of the lungs which is liable to affect workmen who constantly inhale irritating particles at work.

Scotopic Sensitivity Syndrome   A form of visual dyslexia and is related to difficulties with light source, intensity and colour. It is a distinctively different visual problem from visual acuity and refractive errors. Individuals who suffer from it often complain of distortion or movement of black print on a white background.

Special Education Act, 1971

This statute placed the responsibility for the education of all children firmly under the local authority education departments. Previously, those with severe handicaps had been the responsibility of the health departments. Many such children had been left at home with no formal education. Under this new law no child was regarded as ineducable.

Spina bifida

This is a congenital malformation of the spinal canal. In its severe form paralysis and incontinence can result. The damage to the central nervous system can lead to serious physical and mental handicap.

Many of these children also have hydrocephalus or an abnormal accumulation of cerebral spinal fluid (water on the brain) within the skull. The pressure of the fluid can cause damage to the brain. Cases are treated by the insertion of a

	unidirectional valve which drains the fluid off.
SPS	Schools Psychological Service.
Tourette's Syndrome	A neurological tic disorder which is characterised, in its mild form, by involuntary tics and movements and, in advanced cases, by large involuntary bodily movements, noises like barks and whistles, and in many instances an uncontrollable urge to utter obscenities.
Victorian authoress	The reference here is to George Eliot (1819–1880) – real name Mary Ann Evans – whose books were centred around the Nuneaton area. The George Eliot Hospital is named in her honour.